Candlelight
Ecstasy Romance®

"THIS IS ALL WRONG, MATT," VELLA SAID. "I NEVER SHOULD HAVE BECOME INVOLVED WITH YOU."

"Vella," he began, "somehow we have got to make this work. I love you too much to let you go."

"You don't understand. I don't want to see you again. I've known nothing but heartache since I met you. Let me go back to my private life."

"You don't mean that," he insisted. "I'll give up politics if that's what you want—if it means not losing you."

"I don't want your kind of life. I could never live in a goldfish bowl with people prying and poking at me because—because I can see what most other people can't. I won't change, and you shouldn't either. Neither of us will ever find happiness being less than what we are."

CANDLELIGHT ECSTASY ROMANCES®

THE TROUBLE WITH MAGIC

Megan Lane

A CANDLELIGHT ECSTASY ROMANCE®

Published by
Dell Publishing Co., Inc.
1 Dag Hammarskjold Plaza
New York, New York 10017

Dell ® TM 681510, Dell Publishing Co., Inc.

Candlelight Ecstasy Romance®, 1,203,540, is a registered
trademark of Dell Publishing Co., Inc., New York, New York.

ISBN: 0-440-18779-6

Printed in the United States of America

First printing—October 1985

To Our Readers:

We have been delighted with your enthusiastic response to Candlelight Ecstasy Romances®, and we thank you for the interest you have shown in this exciting series.

In the upcoming months we will continue to present the distinctive sensuous love stories you have come to expect only from Ecstasy. We look forward to bringing you many more books from your favorite authors and also the very finest work from new authors of contemporary romantic fiction.

As always, we are striving to present the unique, absorbing love stories that you enjoy most—books that are more than ordinary romance. Your suggestions and comments are always welcome. Please write to us at the address below.

Sincerely,

The Editors
Candlelight Romances
1 Dag Hammarskjold Plaza
New York, New York 10017

CHAPTER ONE

Vella Redding brushed her long black hair over her shoulder and leaned forward on the edge of her tall ebony stool to add some more color to the greeting card she was designing. The picture was a kaleidoscope of swirling brightness which, when one looked carefully, revealed the face of an Indian surrounded by a headdress of brilliant bird feathers.

A playful wind stirred the ash tree outside her tall studio window, causing the slender branches to sway rhythmically. The sun skipped through the dancing leaves, momentarily splashing golden highlights on the painting.

Just as Vella made the last stroke with her brush, the man's face altered before her eyes. The vision was brief but vivid, as she saw the image of a stranger superimposed over the Indian face she had come to know as well as her own while she painstakingly created it.

Compelling blue eyes replaced the dark Indian ones, and the complexion became fair, the features patrician, yet sensual. Then, as quickly as the face had come, it was gone.

Vella shivered involuntarily and straightened on her stool. She wasn't frightened by the vision; there had been others similar to it over the years and she had become accustomed to them, but this one always left her with a strange, incomplete feeling. She wanted to hold the image longer, to study the picture until she understood why she kept seeing it. But that was never possible.

Because she had seen the same picture periodically since she was a teenager, the man had almost become like a friend, so familiar was his face; yet Vella didn't know him. The visions of him were becoming more frequent now, the details of the face more precise. Still, he remained a mystery to her.

Seeking answers she knew she would not find, she gazed around at the Indian decor which reflected her half-Indian heritage. This room always made her feel good. The floor and walls were decorated with Indian rugs collected from all over the Southwest, each with special meaning; huge pillows covered in brilliant colors were scattered on the floor; and everywhere there were woven baskets, pottery jars, and Kachina dolls.

Vella stared at each of the dolls as if she expected the familiar face with the blue eyes to surface on one. But it did not return.

Abruptly, the phone rang, startling her out of her reverie, causing her to jump in surprise. Her thoughts instantly turned to her close friend, Debby, and for a moment, her total concentration was focused on the woman. Debby's presence seemed so real that Vella could almost touch her.

Reaching out for the phone on her desk, she said, "Hello, Debby."

"Vella, one of these days you're going to speak to the wrong person and be embarrassed," Debby said.

Vella laughed softly. She doubted it seriously,

and she knew Debby did, too. She had known it would be her friend on the line. Obviously she was acutely sensitive today.

"So, what are you up to? It's some new man you're trying to hook for me, isn't it?" she asked.

As sure as the seasons changed, in the springtime Debby began to think of June and weddings, and like a rite of spring, she sought out a husband for her friend. She couldn't seem to tolerate the fact that Vella remained single.

She heard the bright laughter in Debby's voice. "Really, Vella, you're impossible. I just called to invite you to a party."

An image of the man Vella had seen briefly on her painting flashed into her mind, holding her attention momentarily until she spoke again. "What kind of party? Is it for a friend of yours this time?"

There was a slight pause in the conversation before Debby continued. "Not a friend, really. He's a politician. Sam and I are giving a dinner party as a fund-raiser for him. Oh, do say you'll come."

"Not a fund-raiser, Debby," Vella said with a groan. "You know I hate those."

"I'm a little nervous about this one myself," the other woman confessed. "The man is really quite intriguing, and I know he's the best Republican candidate for senator, but something about him intimidates me a little. He's so—so in control. On the other hand, that's what this state needs. He's honest, forthright, and down-to-earth."

Vella thought to herself that he was a rare bird indeed if he was honest and thought he could survive in politics, but she didn't say that. She always

11

stayed strictly away from that topic and she hoped her friend wasn't going to talk politics now.

"Well, at least you're not up to your old match-making tricks," she said to change the subject.

"Oh, not with this one," Debby agreed. "Even I, the eternal romantic, know that this man's not for you." She chuckled ruefully. "Although I'll admit I do hate to pass up the chance to play cupid with such a fascinating specimen. But it would be a disaster of the first order. He was a military man, a war hero, and he'll make a formidable politician."

Vella couldn't miss the excitement in her friend's voice. "He's certainly got strong backing from former political leaders here in the area. I've heard he was handpicked and coached by a retired general he once served under. The movie folks here are mad about him, too. People actually asked us if they could come to the party to show their support. We couldn't say no, but that's why I need you to give me a little support. It promises to be a hectic evening. Please say you will. I'd do it for you if you asked."

Vella's laughter sparkled. "You know I wouldn't give a political fund-raiser if my life depended on it."

"You know what I mean," Debby said in a pleading voice. "I'd do anything at all to help you, and I need your help with this."

Vella suddenly felt a familiar shiver race over her skin. She sensed that she should go to this party; and she had to concede, at least to herself, that the guest of honor did sound intriguing. She was curious to see this man who had her friend in such a dither. It wasn't at all like Deb to be uneasy with anyone. And besides, Vella couldn't refuse such an earnest plea.

12

"When and what time?"

After Debby told her and she had hung up the phone, Vella stared blankly at the painting in front of her, the Indian's face now clear and untainted by the face of the vision. Idly, she wondered why she had let herself be persuaded to attend the party. She disliked those political affairs and she was uncomfortable with the strangers who came to them.

But she had had little choice. She couldn't let her friend down. She adored Debby and her husband Sam; they were energetic and interesting, and seriously dedicated to their political causes. Vella had long ago given up trying to explain her jaded views of politics and politicians. At thirty, she had made it her business to know herself and she had no illusions about her prejudices and preferences.

Catching a movement in her peripheral vision, she looked down just in time to see the tail of her cat as it vanished behind the partially open door. She smiled to herself as she silently followed the multicolored animal. Sneaky was a stray who had seen an easy touch and simply sneaked into her house one morning while she was outside picking up her paper. When she walked past the door, he jumped out to wrap his front paws around Vella's leg, but she had anticipated his move.

"Attack!" she cried, bending down to scoop him up in her arms. She smiled as she gazed into his wide blue eyes.

"You were trying to pull a fast one on me, weren't you?" she said, shaking his big head. She studied the playful cat for a moment, then sighed. "If only you knew how uncomplicated your life is, Sneaky," she told him, thinking of the party.

The large animal began to purr happily. Feeling resigned, Vella went down the cool, dark hall to her bedroom to see what she could wear to the big event.

A week later, Vella drew in a long breath as she paused on the winding walkway of the exclusive house perched high on a hill overlooking the city. Although it was evening and a roguish breeze teased the land, the desert community was still heavy with the day's spring heat. May was barely here, but in Southern California that often meant temperatures in the nineties, and today had been such a day.

There was an aura of gaiety and excitement surrounding the house, and Vella was drawn forward as if being pulled by invisible strings. Glancing at the windows, she watched the silhouettes of the guests as they played across the shades, animated and larger than life.

Suddenly, she trembled with anticipation. She had a feeling that something special was going to happen tonight, and she had never been wrong. Even as a child, she had sensed events that were going to occur before they did. Her mother had encouraged her to trust her intuition, and it soon became clear that Vella's intuition was highly developed.

As though she were already a part of the party, she let the happy atmosphere envelop her when she went up to the front door. She found it odd that she was so eager to join the fun. She really did love a good time, but these political affairs were usually boring. She avoided such occasions whenever possible. And yet, she was looking forward to meeting these people tonight.

"Vella!" Debby spied her friend through the elaborate screen door and hurried forward. "I'm so glad you're here," she said, her face flushed, her eyes glowing. "Come in."

The smile on Vella's face belied the slight tension coursing through her slender, regal body. When she had entered and accepted her small brown-haired friend's kiss, she murmured, "You certainly have an august-looking group tonight."

"I know. The guest of honor really brought them out," Debby said in a low voice. "Now you know why I needed you here for moral support. Just wait until you meet him. His handshake alone is enough to make somebody pay attention to him and his political views."

"One of those, huh?" Vella murmured, thinking of all the hearty, phony politicians she had seen in her time.

"Just wait," her friend said in a low voice. "You'll see." She smoothed the skirt of her gown. "Can you believe it? I, the hostess, didn't know what I should wear to this party."

She lowered her voice even further and whispered conspiratorially, "You know this is an ambitious undertaking for me. The mayor is usually the most important politician I give parties for. I'm so nervous. I had a devil of a time deciding what dress to put on."

Vella laughed. "You managed to find something. You really do look marvelous tonight."

"And you—oh, Vella, must you always outdo us all? It's so unfair," Debby half-joked. "You're already such a magical, mystical creature with your grace and power and looks. Must you dress the part, too?"

She gestured toward the long, sheathlike white

15

dress Vella wore. It clung to her slender figure, outlining her high, pointed breasts and calling attention to the long legs that went with her five-foot-eight-inch body. The dress had a cowl neck in front and was backless. It truly did take an exceptional body to wear it well, and it fit Vella as if it had been made especially for her.

Vella smiled, and her smile had a wonder all its own, sweet and sincere, but her smoke-colored eyes were glinting mischievously.

"You have no worries, Deb. No man will notice me with you standing there in that daring magenta gown. I'd have to do bust exercises for two years to get that cleavage."

Debby giggled. "I have to *scream* my attractions." She glanced down at the V of her dress. "Look at this. It goes all the way to my navel, but you—you're just you," she said, sighing in resignation.

Vella really wasn't aware of how unusual her looks were. She was not beautiful in the classic sense, for her features were too extraordinary, her bone structure all angles and planes, and her coloring so dramatic that she stood out everywhere she went. Straight midnight hair cascaded down her shoulders to contrast with her fair skin, and startlingly wide gray eyes gazed beneath winged brows and thick black lashes.

Her movements were swift and sure, yet she seemed ethereal when she walked. She was so remarkable that most men instinctively shied away until they got to know her.

But that wasn't the case with Matthew Colridge, who sat across the room from her, watching the vision in white with interest. She was the most

16

stunning creature in a room full of stunning crea-
tures, some exquisite, like this woman, and some
simply outrageous, their outfits so outlandish that
they appeared brazen in their attempts to out-
shine the others.

Matt leaned back against the sofa cushions, listening with one ear to the praise several of his
supporters were lavishing on him, trying not to be
obvious about his interest in the lovely woman
across the crowded room. No one watching him
would guess that he was less than the epitome of
the relaxed party-goer, in his element among the
rich and the beautiful, but his twenty years in military service had honed his senses to a fine edge. He
had seen action in Vietnam early on and, most
recently, in Lebanon.

He knew about life and death, and he knew how
to get what he wanted. Tomorrow he wanted a
political career. But tonight—tonight he just
might want the woman across the room. There
was something exceptional about her, something
striking that stirred him like no woman he had
seen in a long, long time, and he had seen many in
his thirty-nine years.

Debra Wright had taken the woman's hand, and
they were coming in Matt's direction. He politely
excused himself from the group of people he had
been talking to, stood up, and reached for a fresh
drink as a waiter worked his way through the
crowd. Then he gave his attention to a petite
blonde who was smiling openly at him, making no
attempt to hide her interest.

"Enough about us," Debby said to Vella. "Let
me introduce you to the guest of honor. I know
how you feel about politicians, so I won't expect

you to chat for long, but you must meet him, of course."

"Of course," Vella agreed. "And I promise I'll ask only polite questions."

"Believe me, this is not the kind of man who can be engaged in answering polite questions," Debby said. "He's not your usual baby-kissing politician. He's charming, but he's dedicated and sharp. He won't be wasting his time or yours with trite conversation."

Vella raised her brows, suddenly interested in meeting the man. She had never known a politician who didn't deal in double-talk and idle party chatter in an effort to win a vote. Even as she thought this, a vision filled her mind. In it, Vella saw herself with a tall man of unusual proportions. The vision was vague and misty, but she and the man seemed to be suspended in midair somewhere. She had a sensation of height and splendor, and incredible excitement. She was sure the man's face was the same one that had briefly obscured her Indian on the greeting card she had been working on. But once more, the vision vanished before she could study it.

She had a strange feeling inside, as if her excitement were building to an explosive crescendo, causing a tightness in her chest and a breathlessness that overwhelmed her. Then, to her shock, as she and Debby worked their way through the crowd, she saw the familiar face of her vision on a man standing across the room.

"My God! It's him!" she gasped aloud involuntarily.

"What?" Debby asked.

Vella shook her head, trying to free it of the image, wondering if she were caught between the tangible and the intangible, transferring the image from her mind to the man in front of her.

But he was all too real, she realized as she stood still, trying to stop the whirling room and get control of her thoughts. Or was it only her mind that was spinning?

Now she understood why she had felt she had to come to this party, and she was wildly excited at the prospect of meeting the man who had already become a part of her life. Still, she couldn't make herself move.

"Come on, Vella," Debby urged, seeing that her friend had stopped right in the middle of the room. "I want you to meet Matt."

Suddenly Vella was weakened by the feeling of distress that spiraled up inside her. The man she had seen couldn't be the guest of honor, the senatorial candidate. Fate couldn't be that cruel. He couldn't be the man in her vision.

But she soon saw that he was. Her heart beating madly, she went with Debby until she was, unbelievably, standing in front of Matthew Colridge, candidate for the U.S. Senate: the man from her waking dreams.

Debby was right, she told herself as her gaze raked over him. He was very unusual, at least in appearance.

Over six feet three inches tall, he towered above both women. Vella wasn't used to that. In her heels, she stood five feet eleven, and that usually put her on a par with most males.

Dressed in a smart navy suit, a pale blue shirt which outlined his sturdy masculine form, and a dark paisley tie, he looked to be in his middle thirties, but Vella correctly guessed that he was closer to forty. His eyes were a deep and penetrating blue and his close-cropped hair was black, sprinkled with gray. He was very muscular, weighing about 210 pounds. His face was lined around the eyes and mouth, and Vella felt certain that he had known much pain.

She was aware of the gaiety and din all around her, but now, before this man, she suddenly experienced the strangest sensation, as if she were standing in the calm before a storm. The noise and laughter all around her seemed to fade away and the image of the other guests blurred so that only the man was clear and vivid.

She felt as if she had finally gotten the answer to some incredibly intriguing puzzle. Standing expectantly before him, smiling warmly, she waited for some response, some sign of recognition from him. She expected him to make the next move, to speak to her, to embrace her, to acknowledge her.

Then it dawned on her that, although she had seen his face a hundred times, he didn't know her at all. She was taken aback to realize that she was the stranger, not he, and she was suddenly bewildered and didn't know what to do or say.

An eternity seemed to pass while she was held captive by his mesmerizing blue eyes before Debby made the introductions.

"Arvella Redding, this is Matthew Colridge."

"Matt," he said, smiling winningly at her. Flashing blue eyes assessed her, seeming to stroke her face with a bold yet flattering intimacy.

Struggling valiantly to get control of herself, Vella shook the hand he held out to her. His touch had a devastating effect, blurring her senses, when she was trying so desperately to control her runaway emotions and behave as if this were an ordinary introduction.

20

Her pulse was racing and her heartbeat hammering in her ears. When she looked into his eyes, she thought that surely she was drowning in them, being swept away by their incredible blueness. Although she was embarrassed by her inability to grasp reality and hang on to the here and now, she couldn't help herself.

She couldn't seem to read this man as clearly as she could other strangers, and she was acutely aware that, even though she had always seen his face, she really knew nothing about him. He was an alluring mystery, and she could no more ignore the sensations he was creating within her than she could ignore the man himself.

When the whirlwind of her reactions finally subsided enough for her to think clearly, she realized that Matt was still holding her hand. The vibrations she felt shocked her as she quickly slipped her fingers from his.

This man was not ordinary political timber, and he had a determination unlike any she had encountered in a long time. Perhaps not since Calan, she told herself. But she quickly suppressed the thought. Calan was a man from another time, another place.

"I'm Vella to my friends," she told Matt, wanting to break the odd spell that bound her to him.

"I hope I'll be your friend," he said, his voice deep and warm. "I'd consider it a pleasure." He smiled. "And I hope you're a registered Republican," he added with a playful twinkle in his eyes.

Vella reminded herself that this man was a politician, skilled in wooing voters and charming women. She found him absolutely delightful and terribly attractive; it wasn't at all like her to be taken so suddenly with a man. But this man was different, she told herself.

Briefly, she was sorry she wasn't politically active and hadn't come here in her enthusiasm to support him. But the thought was fleeting.

"I'm not into politics, Matt," she told him frankly. Then she glanced at Debby, realizing she had been so entranced that she had forgotten the woman standing silently at her side. "I'm here because I'm a friend of the hostess."

Vella thought she saw the faintest flicker of disappointment in Matt's eyes, but perhaps she only wanted to think it.

"I understand," he said. Then, to Vella's surprise, he talked politely with her for a few more minutes, turning the conversation to Debby and Sam as easily as if the party were being given in their behalf.

She was enjoying chatting with him when several people came up to them, eager for an introduction to the guest of honor. After Debby had taken care of the formalities, Vella watched as the circle of people surrounded Matt, seeming to swallow him up in their midst until Debby and Vella had been excluded from the group.

Debby smiled, raising her eyebrows as she looked at her friend. "I'll take you around and introduce you to some of the others you haven't met."

Matt gave the two women a bright smile as they left, but Vella found herself experiencing an unreasonable surge of disappointment that Matt's attention had been claimed by the others. Her mind was still on the politician as she was introduced to a couple nearby. She glanced back over her shoulder and saw that several more people had crowded around Matt and were talking animatedly. Vella gazed at him, able to see his face clearly over the heads of the others, and when she unexpectedly met his eyes, she felt herself flush warmly.

"Vella," Debby whispered behind her hand, "surely that's not Matt you're making eyes at."

The tall brunette looked at Debby in surprise. "I beg your pardon?"

"I said surely you're not making eyes at Matt."

"Don't be silly," Vella replied in a gently chiding tone. "I was impressed with the man, but I'm not personally interested in him." The lie almost choked her, but she forced a smile.

Debby seemed to be genuinely relieved. "I'm glad. Honestly, Vella, two people more opposite than you and him may never have lived. He's against everything you're for and vice versa, from what I've learned of him."

She smiled at her friend. "Besides, he's like a political guru. If you watch him tonight, you'll see that everyone he meets seems to fall under his spell, especially the women."

Vella smiled, but she was a little alarmed to think that she had been so easily seduced. She *had* fallen under the spell of Matt's hypnotic blue eyes.

Suddenly she recalled Debby saying that his handshake alone was enough to make people pay attention to him. She had thought him extraordinary when he took her hand in his, but she had *sensed* his ability, his dedication, his ambition. And she had been overcome by the fact that he was the man in her visions.

"I can understand why. He's quite handsome, and he really is charming," Vella admitted. "But then that's a necessary ingredient in a successful politician, isn't it?"

Debby nodded as she and her friend walked toward a couple who were both weighted down with jewels.

"I know," Vella said quietly before they reached the couple. "Mr. and Mrs. Diamond."

Debby giggled. "Vella, you're awful. You really are," she murmured.

Matt tried to keep his attention on the guests around him, but he found himself thinking what a pity it was that Vella wasn't here because she was interested in politics. He really liked what he saw and the few minutes he had talked with her had revealed her to be warm and sensitive.

She was vital and interesting, and clearly devoted to her friends. He liked that. He realized that he wanted to know more about her. Maybe he could interest her in his new profession.

He suppressed that thought as quickly as it had come; he had learned a long, long time ago that one shouldn't try to change people. He had married a young girl when they were both eighteen, but as weeks passed, he had found they weren't at all compatible. By the time he learned that he couldn't shape someone else as he wanted her to be, it was too late for the brief marriage to be saved.

After that bitter, intense experience, he had remained single for eighteen years. Now he was ready to marry again. He wanted a wife; he needed someone, not just because he knew what an asset the right wife could be in his career, but because he was lonely. The military life had been a nomad life, devoted to school and career, but now he wanted love and stability.

For precisely those reasons, he already suspected that Vella Redding was the last woman he should be attracted to. She had said up-front that she was not interested in politics. Still, as he stared at the dark beauty, he experienced a feeling he couldn't explain, a longing somewhere inside him, an ache that had never quite been sufficiently soothed.

He exchanged a few more words with those around him, then politely but firmly excused himself. As though he were drawn to Vella by some invisible force, he sought out a waiter and took another glass of champagne from his tray. Then he walked over to the two women and waited for Vella to be introduced to the elderly couple with all the diamonds. Reison was their name, he remembered. He was very good with names.

"Vella," he said, relishing the smooth, rich sound of her name on his lips as she and Debby walked away from the old couple.

Smiling, Vella turned to face him, and Matt drew in his breath when his eyes met her entrancing gray ones. He held out the fresh drink.

"I thought you might like a drink." He winked at her. "I hope you don't avoid champagne as well as politics."

Her melodious laughter pleased him. "A girl has to have some vices," she joked as she accepted the glass. She felt the warmth of his fingers as they briefly touched hers, and she heard Debby sigh softly beside her.

"Well, I'll see to my other guests," the small woman said, but her eyes told Vella that she was making a mistake with this man.

Vella squeezed her friend's hand. "I'll talk to you later, Deb."

"May I lure you out on the patio for a breath of fresh air?" Matt asked, feeling foolish. It sounded like a line out of a movie, but he wanted to spend a few minutes with her alone. He had to see what she was made of and why. He really wanted to know, and he knew he wouldn't rest until he had talked with her privately.

"Is it safe?" Vella teased. "I've heard awful tales about you wicked politicians." But even as she teased him, she was working her way through the crowd to the patio doors. She couldn't help but feel flattered because he wanted to escape from the others and spend some time with her alone.

Matt laughed deeply. "I'm not making any campaign promises that I can't keep." He had meant it as a joke, but when she looked back over her bare shoulder at him, he was suddenly seized by a desire to take her in his arms and hold her tightly against him.

As Vella stared into his eyes, she briefly forgot all about the others in the room. For a fleeting moment, she tied into some wavelength that existed only for this man and her, and the message was powerful, though purely physical. She was shaken by it.

Quickly, before she could change her mind about going outside with him, she opened the door with trembling fingers and slipped out. She knew she was behaving imprudently; Deb was right. Vella knew in her heart that she could never be compatible with a politician; there was no point in starting something. But she could no more refuse to go outside with this man than she could fly.

CHAPTER TWO

After being inside the crowded house, Vella found the air deliciously refreshing, and she was glad to step out into the darkness. She needed desperately to shake off the magic web Matt had thrown over her, capturing her as surely as if Debby hadn't already warned her about his charms. The breeze ruffled her hair and clothes and she breathed deeply, relishing the cooling effect. She knew the patio well, for she had often lunched with her friends out by the pool.

Light spilled through the lace curtains on the patio doors, muted and patterned, giving the surrounding area a strange, irregular glow. A crescent moon reluctantly offered its scant scattering of yellow. The pool lights added to the eerie golden brightness, silhouetting Matt as he led the way to a wrought-iron bench. He set the drinks on a small table, then motioned to Vella.

"Won't you sit down?"

She grinned a little at the irony of his invitation. She had known Debby and Sam since college, and she was sure Matt had never set foot in the house until today.

"Thank you," she said, smiling faintly. She was curious to see what he would do now that they were alone. Selecting a seat in the dark shadows of the house, she eased gracefully down on the bench, feeling the coolness of it against her back.

The darkness hugged her, and though she was aware of Matt's powerful presence, he didn't join her. She watched him furtively, seeing him more clearly than he could see her, for he was still in the patterned light. She let the silence grow between them, waiting to hear what this man who dreamed such big dreams would say to her. She sensed that he was here against his better instincts, and she could almost feel him struggling with himself.

She quietly awaited the outcome of the battle, watching as he pretended to nurse his champagne before she finally let her voice drift across the darkness to touch him. "Aren't you going to join me?"

She knew that she had to explore this meeting fully, to see if she could discover why she had seen him so often in her visions. There had to be some reason, but what was it?

"Of course," he said in a smooth voice that sent a shiver over her. With sure steps, he closed the distance between them, breaking the barrier of silence and darkness as he settled down much too close to Vella.

Matt was an impressive man, tall and muscular, exuding power and self-confidence, and he was so damned attractive. Vella once again felt out of control, overwhelmed by his nearness. She eased away from him the slightest bit, hoping the move wouldn't be perceptible in the darkness.

But Matt had given his eyes time to adjust to the blackness, and Vella stood out like a beacon in her white dress against the black bench and dark background. She nervously crossed her legs, and her gown parted to expose long silken curves. The view wasn't wasted on Matt, who eyed her appreciatively.

Vella couldn't help but be aware that he was physically attracted to her, for he made no attempt to conceal it. His gaze rested boldly on her leg, then moved up slowly until it had caressed her hips, breasts, long neck and settled on her face.

"So," he said in a low voice. "Tell me about yourself, Vella. I can't deny that I find you incredibly beautiful."

Vella was surprised by the flutter of her heart. Again she reminded herself that he was used to flattering women, but for the first time in her life, she couldn't seem to keep a practical thought in her head. In truth, she found *him* incredibly appealing, and she was annoyed by her foolish behavior.

"I'm a free-lance artist. I design greeting cards," she told him.

Matt could hear the pleasure in her voice. "What an interesting profession." He smiled, not surprised that she was an artist. He had already guessed that she was warm and sensitive, as well as unusual. "I've never met a greeting card designer before. Is there a possibility I've purchased your work?"

Her gentle laughter spilled out softly into the darkness. "I really don't know. I've been in the business now for nine years, and finally I'm fortunate enough to get my name on my cards. I use a lot of Indian motifs in my work, but of course so do other designers."

"I'd like to see some of your work," he told her seriously, as if it were the most important thing in his life at the moment. "I'll have to look for it now that I know you."

"Does that mean you'll expect me to vote for you?" she asked, her voice light with teasing.

"I can't say I wouldn't like that," he replied, and she could feel his gaze on her. "Are you adamantly apolitical?"

"I'm afraid so," she answered honestly. "I do vote, but that's about the extent of it."

Debby had told her that Matt was forthright; well, so was she, and she wouldn't pretend to have an interest in politics, no matter how attracted to him she was.

For a long time Matt sat beside her in silence, thinking that he should go back inside and leave her while he still could. But he sensed that it was already too late. Despite their blatant differences in attitudes, he was attracted to her; he wanted to get to know her better. He wouldn't leave the topic with that single question. He had never been a man to give up easily.

As he watched her, the moon suddenly seemed to shine down on her, illuminating her like a solitary star, casting a golden hue over her white dress and dark hair. Matt wanted to reach out, to trace her magical form with his unsteady fingers, to draw her to him and understand what it was about her that lured him like a moth to a flame.

It was with amazing restraint that he kept his mind on the subject at hand. "Is it politics or the mere mortals in it who leave you so uninterested?"

Vella thought for a moment before she answered. Her experience with politics had been brief and unsavory. Calan had had his heart set on a political career. Idealistic and visionary, he had honestly thought that the "right" men in govern-

30

ment would change the system, get rid of graft and special interests and corruption.

He had been naive. He had quickly become embittered and disillusioned by what other politicians considered his naiveté and inexperience in a real man's world. So had she, she reminded herself.

Calan, the gentle, sensitive man who had once been her fiancé. He had been only twenty-four and fresh from college with a degree in political science at the time of his entry into the political arena. He had found so quickly that theory was no match for reality.

Vella wasn't even aware of the small sigh that escaped her lips. It had all been years ago, and Calan was only a painful memory now—a promise left unfulfilled. But his venture into government had left its mark on her.

"Both," she said in answer to Matt's question. "It's been my experience that politics is a dirty game, and while I'm sure there are some good men in it, they seem to be in the minority."

Matt was somewhat taken aback by her honesty. However, it certainly wasn't the first time he had heard such remarks.

"Politics *can* be a dirty business," he agreed. "But it's up to us, the citizens, to see that honest men operate our government."

Oh, God, Vella thought to herself, *he can't really believe that. He sounds as idealistic as Calan.*

She couldn't seem to think of any response. She didn't truly even know why she had come out here or what she expected from him. She only knew that his was the face that was so familiar to her, that he was the man she had seen in her visions.

Still, what did it mean? Had she merely seen the

31

face of the handsome stranger she was to meet tonight? Or was there more to it? Was he actually to play some significant part in her life? No, she promptly assured herself. It wasn't possible. But she really wasn't so sure at all.

She wondered what Matt would say if she told him she'd seen him in her waking dreams. Suddenly she recalled how angry Calan had become with her over her visions. Before he had aspired to become a politician, he had been uncomfortable with them, but intrigued, nevertheless.

However, once he had decided to become a candidate, her sensitivity had upset and embarrassed him terribly. He had refused to let her speak about her strange knowledge of things beyond his understanding. She became broodingly pensive as she recalled how desperately she had pleaded with him to listen that last time. But Calan had refused.

Vella's attitude was worse than he had thought, Matt told himself. He was a good soldier; he knew when the war had been lost. He should go back inside.

But ever since he had seen her, he had experienced a strange sense of the inevitable. There was no way to explain it, for he didn't believe in fate. Man made his own destiny.

But this woman attracted him as no other. Just once, he had to know how she felt in his arms, how she tasted to his mouth. Without quite realizing what he was doing, driven by an instinct he could not deny, he drew her to him and his lips claimed hers fiercely, hungrily. For a short eternity, he held her to him, savoring the wonder of her, unwilling to walk out of her life as quickly as he had walked into it.

Vella was surprised by the kiss, but she was powerless to draw away immediately. Her mind told her to flee, but she felt so right, so natural in his arms that she couldn't make herself protest. She let herself be drawn against him, her softness molding to the hard lines of his body.

Her blood raced through her veins with a warmth that sent her temperature soaring. Matt's mouth burned against hers tantalizingly, setting a fire in her soul that she knew only he would ever be able to quench. Her blood raced hotly with the heady response to his touch, and she allowed herself a moment to enjoy the intimacy before she pushed at his shoulders with reluctant fingers, turning her head to avoid his persuasive lips.

"You don't believe in wasting time, do you?" she asked in a breathless voice. She couldn't recall the last time she had felt so excited in a man's arms. Her heart was pounding and her pulse was throbbing. She didn't want Matt to know how much his touch had stirred her.

Her husky voice triggered an alarm inside him. He was as surprised as she that he had kissed her. But what alarmed him more was how right she had felt in his arms. Now that he had touched her, he recognized the danger involved. He wanted this woman; he wanted her very much. He knew about discretion being the better part of valor in battle, and it was time for him to withdraw before it became too late.

"Believe it or not, I don't kiss every woman I meet," he told her in a barely controlled voice, still unable to make himself let her go. He was stunned by the hunger she had unleashed in him, by his

33

barely controlled reaction to her touch. He gazed into her eyes, thinking how easy it would be for a man to lose himself forever in that mysterious gray gaze.

"But I won't apologize for it. I found it too enjoyable," he added thickly.

In fact, he wanted nothing more than to kiss her again, to stroke her soft flesh until she burned with the same hot intensity he was feeling. He ached to know her in the most intimate way, to touch her soul, to become an indelible part of her that she would never forget.

He must be going mad, he told himself, suddenly setting her free from his embrace. An immediate sense of emptiness washed over him, and he stood up abruptly, knowing he must put some distance between him and this magical woman who enticed him so inexplicably.

With a strength he didn't know he possessed, he managed to move away from her. "I'd better see you back inside before I give you justification for your earlier comment about wicked politicians."

Now that he had released her, Vella realized how stunned she was by her response to his kiss. She felt as if she had waited all her life for a man to stir her in such a wondrous way, and yet now that it had happened, she was alarmed by her loss of control, by how completely she had been swept away by her own desire.

With a forced smile, she stood up and walked with him back to the patio doors, refusing to acknowledge the regret she was experiencing. It was best that they join the others. They were wrong for each other, regardless of the powerful physical attraction between them.

But there was no way she could avoid acknowledging how moved she had been by his brief embrace and the touch of his lips on hers. The thought sent a tremor through her as the light and noise of the party enveloped her.

As the couple entered the house, Debby rushed up to them.

"Where have you two been hiding? I've been looking for you everywhere. The caterers are ready to serve dinner."

"We went out for a breath of fresh air," Matt said smoothly without looking at Vella.

Deb glanced warily at her friend, then put on a bright smile. "You and Vella lead the way, Matt. She knows where the dining room is."

"Of course," he said, crooking his arm and offering it to Vella.

She tried to pretend that she didn't feel a rush of excitement as she took his arm, but it was difficult.

As she glided by his side, Vella was acutely aware of the tall, broad-shouldered man and his magnetic effect on her. She knew that Deb and Sam were right behind them, and she had to suppress an urge to look back at her friends for support.

"Dinner is ready," Debby announced as they maneuvered through the crowd of guests. "Come along, everyone." Then she and Sam stepped back to allow the others to follow Matt and Vella.

With relief, Vella saw that she was sitting across the table from Matt, and not next to him. "I'm over here," she said, indicating the name in front of her plate.

Matt smiled. "So you are," he said, relinquishing her.

He politely slid out her chair, and Vella felt the touch of his fingers on her back as she sat down

35

and he moved the chair forward. A shiver raced over her skin and she forced herself to pay attention to the other guests. A blonde motioned happily to Matt.

"You're to sit here, Matt. By me," she said, as if she had received the prize for the evening.

Vella turned to smile in greeting as a man took the chair to her right. It was Dwayne Allen. She knew him well, and she felt a small rush of relief. He would hold her interest during the meal. And when the dinner was over, she would find some reason to escape.

There was no point at all in prolonging her discomfort. And she did feel discomfort where Matt was concerned. It was an impossible situation and the sooner she forgot his handsome face and stirring touch, the better. But she knew in her heart that she would never forget, *could* never forget.

"Vella," Dwayne said warmly, distracting her from her thoughts. "How are you, my beauty? You look especially ravishing tonight. What a treat. I didn't know you were coming. I thought you shunned these political affairs."

Vella fought down an urge to glance across the table at Matt to see if he had heard her admirer's comments. "Debby made a special request," she explained. "How have you been, Dwayne? It's good to see you."

"I've been fine. Business is going great, but we won't talk about business tonight. I'm just so delighted to see you. It's been too long—much longer than I'd like. Where have you been hiding yourself?"

She smiled again. "Same old places."

"Tell me where," he murmured. "I want to go there."

Vella was suddenly uncomfortable with Dwayne's interest, unaccountably embarrassed because of Matt. Dwayne had asked her out in the past; however, she had been involved with another man at the time and had refused Dwayne's invitations. Her gaze strayed over his features.

He was quite attractive, with his auburn hair and dancing green eyes, but once again she saw the face change before her eyes. And once more the face she saw had dark hair and blue eyes.

Blinking to rid herself of the image, she looked at Matt. It had been his face she had seen, all right, as if there had really been any doubt. He held her gaze briefly, then smiled slightly, as though against his wishes, and gave his attention to the woman who had seated herself on his other side.

An older, and obviously very wealthy woman, she was chattering in glowing terms about his campaign and his political aspirations. Vella listened for a moment, intrigued in spite of herself, then turned back to Dwayne when he spoke again.

"You didn't tell me where you're keeping yourself," he murmured. "I really want to know."

"Oh, Dwayne," she teased, "surely you don't want to add me to your list of lady friends." A well-known attorney, he was famous for dating his rich clients.

"Don't you kid yourself," he whispered. "I can't remember when I didn't want you."

His serious tone surprised her, and she was relieved when the last guest was seated and a waiter began to fill the glasses with white wine.

Sam stood up. "A toast," he announced. "To Matthew Colridge, our next senator."

There was much clapping and clinking of glasses

as the others saluted Matt. He grinned broadly, then rose to accept the toast.

"Speech, speech," several people cried.

A broad grin played on Matt's full lips, and Vella remembered how wonderful they had felt against her own. She fought to concentrate on something else and listened as Matt spoke.

"Thank you all for coming," he said sincerely. "And for believing in me. I promise I won't disappoint you."

Somehow, Vella suspected that he wouldn't. He was bold and confident, and no doubt quite capable. She felt an absurd flush of pride at knowing him.

When he sat down, he looked at her again. She acknowledged him with her wineglass. "I wish you much success," she said softly.

He met her eyes, surprised by her words, for he knew how she felt about politicians, yet he also knew that she was sincere in her good wishes. Their gazes held for a moment, then someone said Vella's name.

Tearing her eyes away from Matt, she looked past Dwayne and saw a big woman dressed in a lavish purple dress. "Well, hello, LaVerne," she responded warmly, happy to see another familiar face. "I didn't know you were interested in politics."

LaVerne Morris winked. "Not me—George. And he thinks that man across from you is really something. Of course, he was a war hero, and you know how George feels about war heroes."

Vella smiled. She had heard George talk about the Second World War so often she could repeat the stories herself. "Yes," she said.

"But never mind about that." The woman

leaned forward and lowered her voice so that it almost became lost among the others. "I just wanted to thank you for what you did for Judy. She was so upset that she was sick with indecision. Thank God, she didn't take the job. The company relocated just last week—to Montana! It would have been awful if Judy had given up her job for that one."

"I'm glad I could be of some help," Vella replied quietly. "And you're most welcome."

Vella recalled the night Mrs. Morris had called her, desperation in her voice. Her daughter, Judy, had been offered a job with a new company, but there was the possibility of the company relocating.

Judy and her husband had quarreled bitterly about the career change that Judy wanted to make because of the considerable increase in salary, but her husband had been against it. He had been afraid she would lose her job altogether, for he couldn't give up his to follow her if the company moved, and they needed two incomes to meet their financial obligations, which included a sick child.

When Vella had meditated on the problem, she had seen a cloud over a structure, and she had watched as it totally enveloped the building until it was swallowed up completely. She had taken the vision to mean that the company would move, and she had told Mrs. Morris about it.

Judy had turned the job down, grateful to be rid of the decision. Vella had been glad to set the young woman's mind at ease, and now she was pleased that she had given the right advice. She picked up her glass and took a sip of her wine,

unaware that Matt was watching her with renewed interest.

She had obviously helped the other woman in
some way, Matt understood, surprised to find himself eavesdropping on Vella's conversations. He
had heard the man flirting, too, and he had been
amazed to feel a slight flare of jealousy. It had been
ridiculous, of course.

He had always found jealousy a negative, destructive emotion, and it seemed utterly absurd to
apply it to a woman he had met half an hour ago
and would probably never see again. He gazed at
Vella. Damn, but she was lovely. And worse, he
really liked her.

Before he could become lost in his thoughts of
her, he made himself listen to the question the
blonde beside him was asking. The woman glowed
when he answered, and he forced himself to concentrate on the conversation at hand.

Vella looked up as a waiter offered her a portion
of lamb. "No, thank you," she said, but she accepted helpings of each of the vegetables.

"Let me guess," Matt said, almost unaware he
had actually spoken the words on his mind as he
looked over at Vella. There was nothing to do but
finish the statement. "You don't eat meat either."

Vella smiled at him. She had been a vegetarian
all her life. "You're right," she said. "I don't."

Matt groaned inwardly, then forced a smile and
took a large serving of the lamb as a waiter came
up to him. He didn't know why he was instigating
conversation with Vella again. They obviously had
nothing—absolutely nothing—in common.

But that didn't stop him from finding her incredibly intriguing. There was something dis-

40

turbing about her, about the intensity of her gaze, her fathomless gray eyes. He found it very hard *not* to stare at her.

He made polite conversation with the other guests, and occasionally he and Vella spoke, when the man on her other side wasn't monopolizing her, but Matt was glad when the sumptuous meal ended. He was uncomfortably aware of her across from him and he felt as if he needed fresh air to clear his thoughts.

At last he set down his final cup of coffee as Debby and Sam invited the guests to adjourn to the patio for after-dinner drinks. Matt didn't want to go back out by the pool where he had spent such a short, enthralling time with Vella. He saw this as his chance to leave.

"I really must be going," he said, "but I want to thank you all once more for coming." He turned to Debby and Sam. "It was a wonderful evening, but you know about my other commitment."

Sam nodded. "It was an honor, Matt. I know we'll be seeing more of you in the future."

Matt stood up and the guests began to shake his hand and chat briefly as they filed out of the dining room. Soon only Matt, Vella, Debby and Sam were left.

"Must you really leave?" Debby asked. "The night is young."

"I have another engagement, and I'm afraid that it's too important to cancel," he explained.

Vella felt a slight surge of regret. An engagement at this hour? Was it with a woman who patiently waited for him? She brushed the thought aside. What if it were? It was certainly none of her concern.

In fact, she found it a little amusing that he had

beaten her to the punch; he was leaving the party before she could. Now she didn't need an excuse to escape from his compelling blue eyes.

"It was most interesting to meet you," she said in a polite voice as she joined her friends on the other side of the table.

Matt took her hand in a brief clasp, long conditioned to responding automatically to such civilities. For a short moment, their eyes held.

"Perhaps we'll see each other again," he said.

"Perhaps," she replied, hoping it would be so, though she knew it was unwise.

It seemed to her that he gazed at her for an unusually long moment, but time had been distorted for her since she had met him tonight. It seemed to stand still, locking them into a world that held them apart from the others. Finally Matt turned to Debby and Sam, breaking the spell.

"Thank you so much for the party. It was delightful." His smooth voice and warm smile were charming, and Vella longed to have them directed at her just once more, but Matt turned away without another word.

Vella felt bereft, unfulfilled, cheated. Was that it, then? Was that all there was to the visions she had had for years? A few brief words? A tantalizing kiss? And then no more?

She drew in a steadying breath. What on earth was the matter with her? Why was she letting Matt get to her?

As he moved away, she followed his broad retreating back with her eyes, and suddenly she saw a vision of herself lying naked on a bed with him, caressing his broad chest. So startling was the image that she opened her mouth in protest.

Debby turned just in time to see the movement,

and Vella quickly closed her mouth. The distraction effectively erased the vision. Still, she was shaken all the same. She had the power, she knew, to see the future, but that sight had been particularly unnerving. She shook her head to clear it as the host and hostess walked with their guest from the room.

"Coming, Vella?" Debby asked, glancing back over her shoulder, but Vella shook her head. Soon they had left the dining room, leaving her alone with her troubled thoughts.

Leaning against a chair back, she exhaled tiredly. She wished she hadn't come here tonight. She didn't need this complication in her life. She was perfectly happy with her job, her house, and her cat for company. She and Cupid had long had an understanding that couldn't be altered by even the best intentions of her friends and her most ardent suitors.

But Matt wasn't among her suitors, she firmly reminded herself. He was a charming stranger who had somehow magically captivated her in a foolish and weak moment. He was a vision—a waking dream—briefly come to life. A dream she had intimately touched. And must now erase from her thoughts, for truly he had no place in her real world.

Surely it couldn't be part of her destiny to become involved with a politician. Hadn't it been enough that her engagement to Calan had ended in tragedy? She couldn't let Matt into her waking world; of that she was certain. But he was still on her mind when Debby returned.

"Come on and join the party," the other woman coaxed. "Most of the guests are leaving now, and soon the others will follow."

It was the last thing Vella wanted, but she needed the distraction of party chatter, and she went with Debby out onto the patio.

But it was just no good. She was feeling vaguely unhappy and out of sorts without quite knowing why. Even the friends she knew and loved couldn't hold her interest right now, and she firmly declined Dwayne's offer to give her a ride home. She had driven her own car to the party, and she preferred to go home alone, despite the lateness of the hour.

At the thought, she found herself wondering again where Matt had gone. She knew she could ask Debby, for Sam had known about Matt's other engagement, but she didn't want her friend to know how much Matt had attracted and disturbed her.

Her mind filled with unsettling thoughts, she stayed only long enough to help Debby clear up some of the mess which wasn't the responsibility of the caterers, despite her friend's protestations that the maid would do it in the morning. Then she walked out into the cooling night air.

It felt good on her face and body, but didn't soothe her turbulent mind. She placated herself by saying that tomorrow she wouldn't even re-member Matt's name, but she knew it was a lie. For whatever reason, he had made a strong im-pression on her, and she knew he couldn't lightly be swept aside.

The ride back to her house did little to restore her peace of mind, and she was relieved when she parked in the spacious detached garage at the side of the house.

The crescent moon was riding high in the night sky, and Vella watched Sneaky as he came running

44

down the walk to greet her. She smiled to herself; she loved this place and Sneaky was her family. The house was at least thirty years old, but it was just what she had wanted. Situated on an acre of land on the outskirts of the city, it was an oasis in the Southern California desert, and she loved it.

In a little better frame of mind now that she was on beloved turf, she walked up on the vine-covered porch and unlocked the front door. The sweet, cloying scent of honeysuckle filled her nostrils, and she smiled again as she stepped inside.

"Hello, hello," she murmured gently, closing the door behind her before she reached down to pick up Sneaky, who had raced inside with her.

"Did you miss me?" she cooed, experiencing a strange need to feel loved and wanted.

He patted at her face with a paw as Vella carried him down the hall to the kitchen. When she turned on a hanging lamp, the room was flooded with brightness.

She sighed as she handed the cat a treat from an ornate pottery jar. Although Vella kept the house closed up all the time and the air conditioner on low, it wasn't as cool as she would like tonight.

Feeling faintly irritated with herself, she strolled down the hall to the living room and turned on the ceiling fan. Then she seated herself in a priceless French chair upholstered in red velvet. She gazed around the room she loved so dearly and, to her annoyance, she found herself wondering if Matt would see the beauty, the treasures she had diligently gathered for her home.

The entire room was done in red and white, from the carpet to the draperies; even the wallpaper was original. She had merely accented it with her own decor. And everywhere she looked were clocks, her passion from childhood. She had every clock she had been able to get her hands on.

Suddenly the cuckoo clock began to sound off at the stroke of midnight, starting a cacophony that was sure to surprise the unwary but which had caused delight to more than one visitor to the unique house.

Vella watched as Sneaky, thinking himself undetected on the mantel, crept carefully among a collection of glass objects to the end, then leaped on top of the cuckoo clock to attack the bird darting in and out of the little doorway.

Vella smiled to herself. Although the cat was poised and intense, he never could catch the bird.

"Come down from there, Sneaky," she said, repeating a phrase she had used a thousand times and knew she would use a thousand more. "You know it's hopeless."

But it wasn't until the clock had ceased its happy tune that Sneaky climbed down. Then he turned his attention to the grandfather clock with Westminster chimes, concentrating on the strong *bong, bong, bong,* until the sound had stopped.

Next he went dutifully to sit before the grandmother clock, listening and watching as the chimes played a different tune. When they had ended, he made the circuit of the living room clocks, spaced a minute apart, and went to stand before the Regulator clock, obviously his least favorite, for it barely merited his attention.

Because Vella had heard the clocks for years, they usually didn't attract her interest, but tonight she was looking at herself and her home through a stranger's eyes—Matt's.

Displeased because she couldn't get him out of

her mind, she pushed back her chair and stood up. What she needed was sleep, for in sleep she would forget that she had met the handsome aspiring politician.

CHAPTER THREE

When Vella had gone down the long hallway and up the red carpeted steps, Sneaky trailing behind her, she went into the first bedroom on the second floor. She switched on the overhead light, a magnificent chandelier with tiers of pale gold candles. It cast a yellow glow over the lovely bed with its gold and white canopy. Vella had purchased it in France, and it was one of her most prized possessions.

She glanced at the exquisite old-fashioned French telephone on her nightstand, and suddenly she had an urge to talk with her mother. Before she thought about it, she had dialed Anne Redding's number.

"Hello."

Vella grinned at the sound of the lively, familiar voice. "Hello, Mother."

"Vella, darling, how are you?" the woman asked brightly. "What a delightful surprise. What are you doing up in the middle of the night?"

Vella grinned. "It isn't the middle of the night for you, Mother. You roam the house until 3:00 A.M., and then you sleep until eleven."

Hearty laughter sounded on the other end of the line. "That's quite true, isn't it? But you're a day person."

48

Now it was Vella's turn to laugh. "Usually, but tonight I couldn't sleep and I just wanted to talk to you. You've been out of town, remember?"

"Yes, of course I remember. Did you get my card?"

"Yes, and I loved it. Anteaters always make me laugh, no matter what the verse says."

"Good. You know how I love to find those funny ones for you. You seem to enjoy the contrast between those and your own cards."

There was a slight pause, then Anne spoke again. "I'm so glad you called, honey. How is your work going?"

"All right," Vella said. Then she amended the statement. "Fine, really. I'm almost finished with the card I've been working on. I'm quite pleased with it."

Vella suddenly remembered the way Matt's face had appeared over the Indian's, and for a moment she fell silent, wondering if she dared tell her mother about Matthew Colridge. If anyone would understand, Anne Redding would.

"Arvella, what's on your mind?" the woman asked perceptively, and Vella started.

"Nothing. Nothing really." She realized that she wasn't ready to discuss Matt yet.

"Well, when am I going to see you, dear?"

"That's why I called," Vella said. "I was wondering if you have any free time. I'd love to visit."

There was the briefest of pauses, and Vella knew that her mother was checking the huge calendar she kept by the only phone in the cramped apartment.

"Of course I want to see you whenever you get a chance to visit. How about day after tomorrow?"

Vella grinned, not at all fooled by her mother's

ready acquiescence. Anne Redding was involved in everything from her various causes to old-fashioned quilting bees. "That must mean your entire week isn't already booked for a change."

Anne laughed. "Tomorrow's pretty full, and actually I do have a women's group coming at three the day after. It's almost time to send the Indian children to summer camp and we're short of funds. But you know I always have time to see you."

There was another pause, and when Vella said nothing more, her mother asked sweetly, "You wouldn't know anyone who would like to support an unfortunate child for two weeks of summer camp, would you?"

Vella gave an exaggerated sigh. "Just a sometimes prosperous greeting card writer, Mother. I'll bring the check when I come."

In truth, she did everything she could to help, for the Indians were more her people than her mother's. She had been born with Indian blood; her mother had only adopted the people as her own. Vella knew how much her heritage made her the person she was, and she was infinitely grateful for it.

Anne's voice was filled with warm appreciation. "You're such a good child, Arvella. So generous and giving. I want to tell you again how much I appreciate your helping people who need it so much—especially psychically. You have a God-given talent and it's meant to be used."

"You know that I'm more than willing to help anyone who actually has a problem and truly needs me. I think it's a trait I inherited from my mother," Vella said softly. "I just won't give readings to the curious for money, no matter how many people contact me."

"Did someone upset you, dear?" Anne asked, her voice full of concern.

Vella shook her head, even though her mother couldn't see the movement. Matt *had* upset her, but in a way she couldn't explain, even to herself.

"No."

"Is there something specific you want to talk with me about, Arvella?"

Again Vella shook her head. "No, not really. I think I'm just feeling lonesome."

"Honey, I don't mean to pry, and you know I want only what is best for you, whatever that is, but don't you think that what you need in your life is a man?" Anne asked guilelessly.

Vella couldn't help but laugh. It was just like her mother to change the subject to that one. She would like nothing better than a son-in-law and grandchildren.

"*You* don't have one," she countered.

"Good Lord, child! I'm too old," Anne replied. "Anyway, I've had my true love, and though it was brief, it was enough to last a lifetime. There will never be a man to replace your father. Now I hold a cause to my bosom and it keeps the fire burning in me. What makes it burn in you?"

Vella flushed as she thought of the brief time when Matt had held her in his arms. The fire had burned then as never before, but she would not allow herself to dwell on it.

"Good night, Mother. I'll see you day after to-morrow around noon."

"Good night, Arvella."

As Vella replaced the phone, she smiled at the indulgence she had heard in her mother's voice.

51

Then the woman's words returned to her mind. Was her mother right? Did she need a man in her life? And was that man Matt?

Trying to keep her thoughts on other things, she changed into a simple black nightgown and lay down on her bed. But as she stretched out, she was reminded that she had no one to share the bed with.

Sneaky jumped up on the pale silk sheet and made his way on silent feet to his mistress. His eyes were wide and adoring, and he slumped down on Vella's legs, purring contentedly.

"No one to share this bed with but you," Vella told him aloud, talking more to herself than to the cat.

Sneaky looked at her curiously, then he closed his blue eyes and lowered his head. In seconds he was asleep; she was left to gaze around the room restlessly. Finally she switched off the light, but even the darkness brought little comfort to her.

Feeling unhappy and discontented, she rolled over on her side, scooting Sneaky out of the way, then she slid her hands up under the two pillows she slept on, and shut her eyes.

But it was deep into the heart of the night before sleep kissed her brow, and when it came, it brought with it the hauntingly familiar vision of a tall, broad-shouldered man with black hair and blue eyes.

Vella was awakened by the ringing of the phone. She gazed around the room, trying to get her bearings. She had slept much later than usual, and she felt drugged and disoriented. She had been dreaming of Matthew Colridge, and even now, with her eyes open, his face lingered in the misty corners of her mind.

Fumbling around on the nightstand for the phone, she saw that it was nine o'clock. Sneaky had long since abandoned her for other pursuits, and sunshine was streaming in through the upper windows.

"Damn," she muttered, fighting to force herself awake. Finally she grasped the phone and pulled it forward as she sat up against the headboard of the bed.

"Hello."

"Hello. Matt Colridge, here."

"Hello," Vella repeated inanely. Only now did she realize how much she had feared that she would never hear his voice again.

"You sound sleepy," he said. "I hope I didn't wake you."

"No," she said, then added, "I mean yes, actually. But it's all right. I should have been up hours ago."

There was a brief pause, and all Vella heard was the hammering of her own heart. She moved the mouthpiece away from her lips, not wanting Matt to hear her ragged breathing.

She waited eagerly to hear what he would say. Had he, like her, found it impossible to forget that they had touched, and kissed, last night? Did he sense the same inevitability of their meeting that she had experienced?

"I phoned Debby Wright and got your number," he said. "I hope you don't mind."

"No," she murmured. "I trust Debby's discretion."

There was another pause, and Vella had the feeling once again that Matt was struggling with himself.

"Vella," he said at last, "I had to call." He laughed gently. "I think you're a witch who's trying to drive me crazy. I hardly slept at all last night. I kept seeing your face in my dreams, and when I opened my eyes, you were still there."

A shiver raced through her. Should she confess how he had haunted her dreams, how even as he called, she had been waking with the image of him on her mind?

He laughed softly again. "I'm afraid you've really captivated me. I know this is short notice, but I'd love to see you tonight—take you to dinner, if that's all right. Are you free?"

Vella's hand closed more tightly around the phone, and she tried to keep the excitement out of her voice. She was behaving absurdly, but she couldn't make herself calm down. She wanted very much to see Matt, and as soon as possible.

"It just so happens that I am free and would love to go with you," she said warmly.

"Will seven be good for you?"

"Yes," she answered.

"Good. I'll see you then."

She had just hung up when the phone rang again.

"Hello."

"Vella, Matt again. I don't know where you live."

They both laughed. Vella was still amused as she gave him her address and directions to the house. She hung up and, smiling to herself, scooted to the edge of the bed. The day was starting out well, very well indeed.

Feeling almost giddy with anticipation, Vella

went to her closet and began to search through her clothes for something to wear to dinner. She had many outfits that pleased her, but she wanted something very special for this evening.

She finally settled on a bright red dress adorned with a bit of fringe on the hem and sleeves. Because it was unusual, it was one of her favorites. She would accent it with some sexy strappy heels and a wide black belt.

Satisfied with her choice, she went downstairs to make breakfast, a lightness in her step. Sneaky came bounding in through the pet door, mewing excitedly when he heard her.

"How are you this morning, kitty?" she asked affectionately, smiling down at him. "Hungry, are you?"

He wound around her legs impatiently as she took a can of tuna from a kitchen cupboard and mixed it with dry cat food. When she had set the dish on the floor, she watched as Sneaky sat quietly on his haunches and began to eat.

When she had prepared her own meal of fresh fruit, yogurt, a boiled egg, and orange juice, she went over to the table and sat down.

Matt was still heavy on her mind, and she knew if she didn't concentrate on something else, the day would drag endlessly for her. The lilies of the valley centerpiece caught her eye, and she studied the potted plant as she ate, trying determinedly to shut out her thoughts of Matt and the evening ahead of her.

The dainty white bells were fragrant and delicate against broad green leaves, and the dark red pail which housed the lilies heightened their air of fragility. Vella studied them thoughtfully, intently. They were her favorite flower, and they grew in abundance in her garden under the sturdy, shading branches of an ancient apple tree.

She was familiar with the legends about them, including the one which suggested lilies of the valley had been created by Eve's tears when she was expelled from the Garden of Eden; she also knew about the magical powers attributed to them, especially those associated with love.

As she gazed at the plant, the wheels of her mind began to turn. Her Indian greeting card would be finished today, and she would begin to work on something new. Perhaps the flowers would be a good design.

Who knows, she told herself, maybe she would even work something in that displayed their aphrodisiac powers. That seemed appropriate, since the verse she was designing the card for was charming and romantic.

Despite her determination, thoughts of Matt overshadowed her thoughts of the flowers as she recalled how he had said he wanted to see some of her work. *Now there was one man who wouldn't need aphrodisiacs to win anyone over,* she thought.

She brushed the thought aside. She couldn't spend the whole day thinking of him. "What you need to do, ol' girl," she said aloud, "is to keep busy."

She finished her meal and was clearing off the table when the phone rang.

"Hello," she murmured.

"Vella," Debby's voice was high and excited. "Did Matt call you?"

"Yes, he did."

"I didn't know if I should give him your number

56

or not, but he was so insistent. I hope you don't mind."

"No," Vella answered truthfully. "No, not at all."

"What did he want? Did he ask you out?"

Vella smiled at her friend's blunt questions. "Yes, we're going to dinner tonight."

There was a slight pause, and when Debby spoke again, her voice was edged with concern. "I sure hope you know what you're doing, Vella. It's none of my business, but I don't see how any good can come of a relationship between you and Matt."

Vella felt a rush of discomfort as her friend's words penetrated. She had deliberately suppressed such thoughts. She had been too pleased to hear Matt's voice, too pleased by the prospect of seeing him again. Now she didn't want to hear the nagging refrain in her head that echoed Debby's worry.

"He didn't ask me to marry him, Deb. He just invited me to dinner."

Debby laughed nervously. "All right, Vella. It's your life. Have a good time, and tell him hello for me—and Vella, call me first thing in the morning. I'm dying to know all about your date."

Vella laughed good-naturedly, but the call had already begun to distress her. "Good-bye, Deb. Thanks for giving him my number."

She hung up the phone, then sat staring at it for a moment. *Did* she know what she was doing? As she had told Debby, she was only going out to dinner with Matthew Colridge. But wasn't she hoping for more than one evening with him? She knew all too well that there was more involved here than a single date with a handsome man. Much more.

She moved away from the phone. How could seeing Matt be wrong when it seemed so right? Renewing her determination to concentrate on her work today, she marched purposefully from the kitchen to her studio on the second floor.

She paused a moment as she stepped inside, trying to get in a more positive frame of mind. She couldn't work if she was agitated. She let her gaze travel around the room, drinking in the Indian decor.

This place soothed her jangled nerves; it made her feel comfortable, as if this were where she belonged. More than any room in the house, this one was home to her. Calmness settled over her as she stood perfectly still for a moment, letting the mood of the room seep into her. It was here that she created the magic that was her work, here that she came to be renewed, here that she felt most at ease.

She sat down on her black stool and began to add the finishing touches to her Indian painting. But try as she might, she couldn't stop thinking about Matt. She had seen his face on this very card —was it only yesterday? It seemed like an eternity ago.

Glancing at the clock, she saw that it was only nine forty-five. There were nine hours left before she would see him in the flesh. She simply had to focus on her work if she were to get through the day.

Forcing her attention back to the card, she made herself concentrate, but her gaze strayed repeatedly to the clock. The seconds turned into minutes, the minutes became an hour, and eventually Vella managed to lose herself in her creation.

Soon the Indian face was completed. As Vella set it aside to be readied for tomorrow's mail, she decided that she was quite pleased with it. Then she gave her attention to her next idea, having already made up her mind that it would feature lilies of the valley.

For a long time she meditated about it, lost in the hidden and secret places of her mind, calling up her creativity until she could see what she wanted as clearly as if it were already a fact. At last she was satisfied with the images she saw and she began the tentative sketches that would eventually be a finished product.

As she worked, she became totally absorbed in the magic that was her creation. The images materializing were already as real to Vella as if they were alive with velvet softness, filling the room with their sweet scent. She became totally absorbed in the flowers, her hands moving instinctively, guided by some subconscious part of her mind. Soon her love for her work transported her beyond the surroundings of the room and she became completely lost in the tiny bells blossoming on her easel.

Vella wasn't aware of how much time had passed until her back began to ache. She straightened up on her stool, stretched, then gazed around the room, slowly coming back to the reality of her surroundings. With surprise, she saw that it was six already. She had missed lunch completely, and if she were to be dressed in time for dinner, she would have to hurry.

When seven o'clock arrived, she was downstairs waiting for Matt. She looked quite stunning in the red dress, her hair done up in a smooth chignon.

The ringing of the doorbell coincided with the

sounds of the cuckoo clock, and Vella went to answer while Sneaky started his evening rounds of the clocks.

She opened the door to find Matt standing before her in gray slacks and a navy shirt which set off his compelling blue eyes. Vella found him even more handsome than she had last night.

"Hello," he said. His penetrating gaze didn't miss anything, and she could see that he was more than pleased with her outfit.

"You look delightful," he said admiringly. "What an intriguing dress. You remind me of an Indian princess in that."

Vella smiled. "I've a penchant for Indian things," she said, leading him inside. "I'm half Indian, you see."

"I didn't know," he said. His eyes were full of interest. "You're a fascinating woman."

He took her hand and held it in his, and Vella couldn't deny the dangerous electricity that sparked within her at his slightest touch. "I'll tell you quite honestly that I hadn't intended to see you again." He shrugged slightly. "After all, you and I seem to be diametrically opposed to each other in so many ways."

Vella couldn't turn away from his hypnotic blue eyes. "I hope that doesn't mean we can't be friends," she said.

But she already knew that she wanted much more than that, and that she was afraid they were starting fires that could never be more than embers left unfed.

He studied her for a moment. "Yes," he said at last. "I think we can be friends."

But he knew he would never be satisfied with only friendship with Vella. Coming to her house like this, being here with her, seemed to be part of his destiny. This place, this woman, seemed to be the goal he had sought at the end of a long, weary road he had ceaselessly traveled. It troubled him; suddenly he didn't seem to be in control of his life.

"May I get you a drink?" she asked, leading him into the living room.

"Yes, I'd like that. Bourbon and water, if you have it," he said, gazing around the room.

When Matt caught sight of Sneaky, who boldly stood his ground in front of the grandfather clock, he laughed.

"This is a wonderful place you have here," he told Vella. "That cat is charming."

His attention was caught by the grandmother clock when its gentle chimes echoed those of the grandfather. His eyes dancing merrily, he glanced back at Vella.

"Do you have the correct time?"

Pleased to see that he had a sense of humor, Vella grinned at him. "I have two passions: clocks of all kinds and antiques."

"Hmm," he said, accepting the drink and sitting down on the couch beside her, "only two. I'm disappointed."

He was smiling playfully, and Vella told herself that he was the most attractive man she had seen in years. She shrugged lightly. "Oh, perhaps a few others—my work—"

"No man in your life who qualifies as a passion?" he asked bluntly. He was still smiling, but Vella saw that his eyes were absolutely serious.

She shook her head. "No, not in a long time," she told him.

Matt thought about it for a moment, more pleased than he wanted to admit. "Maybe we can change that," he said, his tone less light than he had intended.

Vella tilted her head and smiled at him. "Oh?" she asked.

Matt had a strong urge to set his drink down and draw her into his arms. He had not been able to forget, not even when he was sleeping, how she had felt when he kissed her. But he was going too fast. He needed to take his time with her, feel his way.

He sharply reminded himself that he knew so little about her. She was gorgeous, enchanting, sensual, and warm. She was also a little eccentric, judging from what he could see of her house, but then that wasn't at all unusual in an artist.

"Do you allow visitors in your workroom?" he asked, wanting to know more about her.

"Sometimes, if they're interested enough to ask," she said.

"I'd like to see it."

She took a sip of her wine, then set it on the marble table in front of them. "Right this way," she said, standing up.

Matt set his bourbon glass on the table and followed her from the room. As she moved gracefully before him, he saw again how beautiful her legs were. She had been in a long dress last night, and he had had only a glimpse of her legs. Vella looked back over her shoulder in time to see his gaze moving up her shapely body, and she quickly turned back around, for a moment too embarrassed to speak.

When they entered her studio, he gazed around in amazement. "What a great place for your kind of work," he said. "I remember that you said you use a lot of Indian motifs. How inspiring this must be."

His blue eyes met her gray ones. "But, of course, it must be quite natural for someone with an Indian heritage. You'll have to tell me all about your parents and your background."

"Yes, of course," Vella said as Matt moved farther into the room. But somehow she couldn't imagine honestly discussing her background with him. She didn't want to frighten him away with the true tale of a mother who had been addicted to causes and had run off to Arizona to live with the Indians.

Matt gazed around pensively, sensing that this magical room had special meaning to the woman before him—both the Indian and the artist. He felt that he could find her here, get to know her better. And he wanted that very much. If he could begin to understand her, then perhaps he could understand what it was about her that drew him to her so inexorably.

Almost unconsciously he began to touch the collection of baskets, tracing the weave with his index finger, feeling the fine texture of the material. He ran his hands over the rugs, exploring the patterns, studying the many colors. Then he turned to the pottery, gently picking up piece after piece, as if they held the answer to Vella's secrets.

Vella watched him, finding it odd that he seemed so at home in her workroom. Most people peeked inside only long enough to satisfy their curiosity, but Matt seemed intensely interested. He seemed to want to touch and feel and see until he became saturated with the contents of the room. She found his interest quite moving, as though he were establishing some kind of bond with her by understanding her love for her sanctuary. The thought caused her to tremble slightly.

Finally he stepped forward to inspect the sketch she had begun to work on.

"This looks like lilies of the valley," he said, and Vella noted that some of the intensity was gone from his face. He looked like a man who had found some answers.

"Yes, it is," she agreed, going over to stand beside him. She indicated the tall pot on her bookcase. "There's my inspiration."

"Aren't you going to use an Indian design this time?" he asked, particularly fascinated by her Indian heritage.

Her smile was almost mystical. "I'm sure I'll find some tie-in with the flowers," she said thoughtfully. "It just hasn't come to me yet."

Matt straightened when he saw the roughs of the last card she had worked on, the one which featured the Indian. He went over to the completed picture and picked it up.

Vella saw that his face was now completely free of the tension she had seen earlier; his brow was no longer furrowed.

"This is marvelous," he said. "It's quite compelling."

He looked up at her, and suddenly Vella wondered if he could see his own reflection in the picture, as she had done. Her heart beat wildly at the thought, and she fought to control her pounding pulse. But of course, he didn't see himself, she chided her foolish heart. It had been *her* vision; but as her eyes met his, neither one of them seemed able to look away. Vella felt in that moment that they had touched somewhere in a realm beyond this room, thereby establishing a bond that could never be broken.

She remembered how she had first seen his face on that drawing. Now he was here in her work-room, as if he had stepped out of the picture. He was meant to come into her life. She was sure of it. But what now?

"I'm really impressed with your work," Matt said, scattering Vella's thoughts.

"Thank you," she finally managed to say over the swirling thoughts inside her head.

Their gazes held for a moment longer, and Matt was moved in a way he had never before experienced. He felt that he was with someone rare, someone exceptionally sensitive and aware. He couldn't quite explain why, but there was a unique quality about Vella, something he had never found in any other woman he had met, yet he couldn't forget that he hardly knew her at all.

He glanced at his watch. "We should get under way. I've made reservations for seven-thirty. I hope you'll like the restaurant."

"I haven't found a restaurant in Palm Springs that I don't like," she told him with a smile.

"Have you lived here long?" he asked.

"Nine years. How about you?"

"Only a few months. I'm a native Californian, but I lived in Orange County before I went into military service."

"Do you like the city?" she asked.

"What I've seen of it. I've been busy learning about politics since I was discharged. I'd like to have you show me the sights."

She laughed. "I'm sure you have people who could show you much better than I—and give you more information," she insisted.

65

"Maybe," he admitted. "But I'd prefer you."

"We'll see," she said evasively, knowing she was denying the inevitable.

"Good. I'll consider it a date." He stepped aside to let her pass, and he shook his head as Sneaky marched out behind her. "After you," he said to the big tomcat, who had appeared out of nowhere.

Vella glanced back at him, then smiled to herself. Matt certainly wasn't a typical politician; she had been all too ready to stereotype him, and now she was a little dismayed to find that she had been wrong. He wasn't the brash, fast-talking man she had expected; he was warm and amusing, with an innate dignity.

And he was also idealistic, she told herself, remembering how he had said that it was up to the citizens to keep the government honest. But his idealism might well hurt him if he stayed in politics—just as it had hurt Calan.

When she and Matt had settled into his gray Mercedes, she asked, "Why did you get into politics?"

He was thoughtful for a moment. "I learned a lot about people in the service. I also learned about life and death. You learn in war that death is swift and permanent. What counts in this world is what we do right here, right now."

His blue eyes glittered with fire when they met hers. "The poor, the oppressed, the needy, don't care about crystal ball ideology. They want jobs and food and resources, not rhetoric and promises. I think I have something to offer them, and I have every intention of doing that.

"I'm sorry," he added with a laugh. "I didn't mean to make a speech in response to your question. I guess that's the politician in me."

Vella was strangely pained by his pragmatism, his realism. "Don't you believe in the hereafter?" she asked quietly.

He slanted his eyes at her, briefly wondering if she did. "I've seen a lot of good men die—young men—men of hope and promise. I don't know anyone who's died and come back," he said gently. "Do you?"

"Then you don't believe in premonitions, in worlds beyond what we see and touch here on earth, do you?" she asked without replying to his question.

Matt answered immediately. "I hope there's a supreme being, but this world is the only one I know, the only one I can accept."

An uneasy silence fell over the occupants of the car as it wound its way toward the city, and Vella was relieved when she saw the lights. She wanted to shed this feeling of incompatibility, of isolation, to once again see Matt laugh and talk animatedly. She liked him. She wanted to enjoy herself with him. She didn't want to think about politicians or visions—or never seeing him again.

"Here we are," he said, interrupting her troublesome thoughts.

Looking out at the brooding castle which loomed before them, Vella was glad indeed that she had chosen her red dress. The restaurant was a fascinating place, and very exclusive. She had eaten here once before, and she had loved it.

When Matt had come around to her side of the car, he opened the door, took her hand, and helped her out. "How gallant you are," she said with just a trace of teasing in her voice. She wanted desperately to regain their earlier rapport.

67

"It's my natural charm," he joked, winking at her.

It was indeed, she told herself, as he wrapped his arm around her waist and walked with her to the wide front doors of the building. His touch was full of magic, and Vella soon forgot all about the conversation they had had in the car. When he was so near, she could think only of him, of the way he stirred something elemental in her soul, of how her blood sang in her veins with excitement.

She was determined that she was going to enjoy this evening with him. She wanted it to be special and wondrous, as she knew it could be—a night that dreams and memories are made of, a night she could treasure all her life.

CHAPTER FOUR

Vella smiled to herself as she and Matt walked into the restaurant. It was decorated in medieval style, and instantly she was caught up in the dark, mysterious atmosphere. As she gazed around at the heavy tables and chairs and the rustic decor, she told herself that she would like to eat here more often, but her first experience had taught her that it was simply too expensive.

As they were led down the winding halls past many partitioned rooms, her eyes met Matt's. His danced with unusual brightness in the glow of the muted light from wall torches and hanging lanterns, and she could feel the heat from his fingers as they rested lightly on her back, gently guiding her through the dim corridors.

Their footsteps were muted by thick rugs on the floors. On the walls were exquisite many-colored tapestries with designs of castles and dragons and flowing rivers. Vella smiled with delight as they followed the waiter up some narrow curving stairs to the second floor, where they were directed to a secluded table in a corner of the room.

"Is this all right?" Matt asked, pulling out her chair himself to seat her, though the headwaiter hovered nearby.

"Oh, Matt, it's splendid." She gazed around the

dimly lit room, seeing that it held only two other tables. "It has such an aura of mystery and magic." Her eyes sparkled brightly as they met his. "I almost expect sorcerers and kings to dine with us."

Matt's deep laughter revealed his pleasure. "Perhaps they will." He seated himself across from her, and he couldn't seem to take his eyes off her for a moment. "I feel as if I'm already dining with a princess," he said, taking her hands in his.

They turned to look at the headwaiter when he politely told them to enjoy their meal.

"Thank you," Matt said, but clearly both he and Vella had forgotten that the man was still with them.

Another waiter came up for their drink order, and it was with great difficulty that Matt released Vella's hands to take a quick look at the menu. They both settled for an exotic-sounding plum wine, then briefly studied the night's fare. Matt noted with relief that there were selections for a vegetarian.

When they had ordered dinner, they sat in companionable silence for a few moments, sipping the heady plum wine. The long, tapered candle on their table flickered brightly, casting smaller shadows on those already made by the lanterns and torches, surrounding the couple with shadowy images, wrapping them in a little world that held only the dancing reflections of themselves.

Vella gazed thoughtfully at the shaded planes of Matt's face, admiring his strong features and dark blue eyes. She wanted to know all about him, what his life was about, what had shaped his views.

"How old were you when you went into the service?" she asked, her soft voice sounding whispery in the high-ceilinged room.

Matt returned her thoughtful gaze for a few seconds, his blue eyes assessing her fragile beauty in the wavering light. Then he looked down at his wineglass before meeting her eyes again.

He shook his head at some remote memory. "You mean how young and foolish?" His low voice seemed appropriate in the subdued room, in harmony with that of the other diners who were talking quietly among themselves. "I was reared by moderately well-to-do parents who had my future mapped out from cradle to grave."

He grinned boyishly at her and his eyes glowed with mischief. "I'm sorry to tell you that I was a rebellious youth. I never liked anyone making my decisions for me. When I was eighteen I did two foolish things: I married my high school sweetheart and enlisted in the Marines."

Vella was a little surprised that he had ever done anything foolish; he seemed the type to have always known in what direction he was headed. And she hadn't considered the possibility that he might be divorced. She knew that he wasn't married, and she had assumed for some reason that he never had been.

"Do you have children?"

"No, thank God," he said. "At least we weren't that foolish. The marriage only lasted a year." His eyes were a little distant, as though he had never gotten over the failure of his short marriage. "It was an awful mistake. We weren't suited at all, and she couldn't adapt to the life of a serviceman."

"I'm sorry to hear that," she said, understanding that it must have been a painful reality for him.

"We both got over it," he said. "Then I devoted myself to my studies. I obsessively pursued a college education and soon became an officer. Not

71

necessarily a gentleman," he said with a smile, "but certainly an officer."

"I'm sure you were a very fine one," she said, believing it.

"I tried to be," he said modestly. "And what about your childhood? Where did you live? Is your father a member of the local tribe of Agua Caliente Indians?"

Vella shifted uncomfortably in her chair. She sensed that even though Matt was clearly interested in her, he was not yet ready to know about her background. The truth of the matter was that she was illegitimate and her father was a Navajo Indian who had died ten years ago without Vella's ever having known him.

For a brief moment, she slipped back in time as she recalled how fascinated she had been by the story when her mother had told her of running away after college to work with the Indians against her parents' wishes. Vella had always listened enraptured when her mother told her the love story of the young white girl and the handsome Navajo man.

However, it was the old and sad tale of love being unable to cross bloodlines; somehow it made the poignant story even more romantic, and it made her, the proof of the couple's love, feel extraordinary and special. She had been reared on Indian legends and insights, but she had always kept that part of her a secret from even the most reliable of friends.

"My father was a Navajo who lived on the reservation in Arizona," she said. "He and my mother separated before I was born. My mother moved to California, and I never knew my father." She didn't add that her mother had asked that this should be so.

"That seems a pity," Matt said. "Is your mother still alive?"

Vella smiled. "Alive and kicking almost as high as ever. She's been committed to the plight of the Indians since she was young and she still is, even though others abandoned the struggle long ago. One thing about my mother—she doesn't give up."

"She sounds interesting," Matt said, keeping a smile on his face. But he suddenly had a fleeting feeling of unease. The more he learned about this unique, enchanting woman across from him, the more unsuitable she sounded. Realistically—and he was a very realistic man—he knew it was possible that he was playing with fire, courting disaster, both politically and emotionally, but he was already here in Vella's company, and he had no desire to leave.

When he saw the dreamy look in her eyes, he dismissed his troublesome thoughts. How could anything but joy come from knowing this exquisite creature? She was a vision in red, luring him ever closer with her beauty and her charm and her shimmering gray eyes. Every time he looked at her, he seemed to be drawn deeper into the depths of those mysterious eyes. It was as if Vella had cast some kind of love spell on him, and he was a most willing victim, wanting to enjoy every moment of it.

He had no wish to analyze a possible future with her. All his life he had guarded his emotions, and now he just wanted to give in to this magic time and savor it. He had never met anyone quite like

73

her, and it was an experience he wanted to relish while he had the opportunity.

In fact, he wanted to know more about her. Much more. "Have you ever been married?"

She appeared momentarily startled by the question. She lowered her eyes, then glanced up at Matt uncertainly. She seemed to be struggling with some unpleasant remembrance, and when she looked at him again, he was surprised to see a misty sheen on her eyes.

She shook her head. "I came close once, but it didn't work out."

Matt reached out for her hand and locked her fingers in his to squeeze them gently. He had a sudden urge to hold her to him, to comfort her until the haunting ache he saw in her eyes was gone forever.

Vella met his gaze, and for a brief moment, they stared at each other in silence. Clearly she didn't want to elaborate on her answer. The silence suddenly swelled between them until Matt thought he would drown in it. He knew he had to speak before he became hopelessly lost in Vella's pain.

"How did you become interested in art?" he asked, wanting to see her happy again.

The silence seemed to fall away slowly, breaking bit by bit as Vella regained her composure. The unhappy look faded from her eyes and they began to glow as she started to talk.

"Ever since I was a child, I've had all these ideas inside me, these dreams and visions and beautiful thoughts that I wanted to share with someone else. My mother always encouraged me to express myself in every way. At her instigation, I began to put my dreams on construction paper and color them

74

with crayons. My mother exclaimed over them as if they were miracles."

She smiled at the memory, and Matt smiled with her. He considered her a rare and precious woman, and he realized that her mother had had a great influence upon her.

"You must love her very much."

Vella nodded. "She's been a tremendous source of both knowledge and inspiration for me. People have always thought she was a bit crazy, but for me she's simply different and wonderful. She's in her fifties now, and her zest for life has never waned."

"She does sound remarkable," Matt said. "And so do you," he added sincerely.

Mentally, he shook his head. God knows he wasn't a romantic, but he was so taken with this woman, so bemused, that he couldn't seem to think straight. It was as if she had woven a silken web around him with her wonder and her magic, and he couldn't seem to shake it.

The more he heard about her, the more remote she became as a possible wife for him, but the more firmly she entrenched herself in his fantasies. If he weren't a political candidate, he would let himself run wild, learning about her, touching her, both literally and figuratively. He wanted to know all about her—what she thought, what she hoped for, what she believed in.

He was disturbed to realize how enthralled he was. It was much too soon to be so crazy about a woman he hardly knew. After his bad marriage, he had vowed never to rush into love again. His intense response to Vella unsettled him; he was letting his emotions get out of hand. He had always been a man of supreme control, and now he remembered how much he had desired her last night when he kissed her.

He was immensely relieved when their meal was served. The interruption gave him the chance he needed to put a little distance between them. He sat up straighter in his chair and began eating. It was several minutes before he spoke again, and this time he intended not to get so intensely involved in the conversation.

"How is your dinner?" he asked.

"Very good," Vella said. "And yours?"

"Delicious. This sauce reminds me of one that Mother used to make. It was my favorite, and I'm afraid she spoiled me by preparing it any time I asked her to."

Vella smiled. "Do you have any brothers and sisters?"

"No. Funny, sometimes when I was growing up, I felt a little like an outsider, even though my parents doted on me. There were many times when I almost envied my mother and father their close relationship. They've been married forty-two years." He smiled. "It seems like a lifetime, but they're so good together, so dedicated and devoted, and still so much in love."

Vella lowered her eyes, her long lashes shadowy on her face as she traced circles on the moisture coating her water glass. "I'd like that to happen to me," she said. "It must be wonderful. Sometimes I feel very alone."

She looked up at Matt, suddenly embarrassed. What on earth had prompted her to say that? She was perfectly happy with her life. She had chosen to be alone. After Calan, she hadn't wanted to get involved with anyone. This man, this politician, with his charisma and his questions, was making her think—and say—things she hadn't thought in years.

"Love is wonderful," Matt agreed, and he had to fight against telling Vella that he would like to be the one to give her that kind of closeness, that kind of love. She answered some need deep inside him, and here in the dimly flickering light, he was beginning to dream dreams—dreams he had given up much too long ago.

He felt a sudden need to take her away from the restaurant, away from the other people in the room, to have her all to himself. At the moment his greatest wish was to draw her into his arms and make love to her.

It was another foolish thought, he chastised himself. They hadn't even finished their meal, and he doubted very much if she wanted to run out in the middle of dinner just to be alone with him.

"Can we go?" Vella asked abruptly, causing Matt to open his eyes wide in surprise.

She blushed. "I know it's silly, but I suddenly feel very crowded in here."

Matt swallowed with difficulty. Would she think he was crazy if he told her she had echoed his own thoughts? Of course she would, he told himself. It was simply a coincidence. Or was it?

"Yes, we can leave," he told her. "All of a sudden, I find that I'm not very hungry. I had thought of asking if you would mind leaving." He waited expectantly to see what she would say, and he was strangely disappointed when she didn't reply. For a moment, he had thought that they had read each other's minds.

He shook his head. He really was going mad; there was no doubt about that. It was for the best that he take her home now. He needed some time to think, to consider her in more realistic terms. He was overwhelmed by his attraction to her.

The return ride was conducted in a strange kind of anticipatory silence. Both Matt and Vella seemed lost in their thoughts. The car was filled with an electric tension, but now that they were outside the magic atmosphere of the restaurant, reality had crept in.

As Vella gazed out at the night scenery, she told herself that Matt must think she was crazy. She didn't know what had prompted her to leave the restaurant right in the middle of dinner. Suddenly she had been overcome by a desire to spend time with him in private. Now she was embarrassed by her impulsive behavior.

When Matt had parked in front of the house, he walked around to Vella's side to open her door. En route, it occurred to him that she might have wanted to leave the restaurant because she wasn't enjoying herself. He didn't know why he hadn't considered it at the time. Funny, even now he found the thought intolerable. Although he needed a little respite from the rush of emotions that had overpowered him in the two days he had known her, he couldn't imagine not seeing her again.

After he had walked her to the door, the two of them lingered awkwardly for a few minutes. Matt gazed at Vella expectantly. She was beautiful in the moonlight, her gray eyes shining brightly, her pale face lovely. He knew he couldn't leave without kissing her, but he wasn't sure he had the willpower to stop with a single kiss. He was afraid that if he took her in his arms, he would never want to let her go.

He stared at her, thinking that he should tear

himself away, but somehow lacking the strength. He was hungry for the taste of her, the feel of her. He fought furiously with himself, and it was with no little measure of self-control that he drew her firmly to him to claim only a single kiss from her gentle lips.

The touch of her mouth, warm and tender against his own, caused a warmth to cover his skin. He was breathing raggedly when he raised his head and gazed down at Vella. As he had feared, one kiss only drove him to want another.

But he would surely be lost if he gave in to the impulse. He really didn't know what was wrong with him. He was a man who had survived wars, who had made decisions and led other men. And yet he couldn't seem to keep a sane thought in his head when he was with this mysterious woman with her compelling gray eyes and dark beauty.

He was trembling with the force of his self-restraint when he pulled her closer with a groan. He hugged her to him for a moment, then held her at arm's length, looking deeply into her eyes.

There was a brief pause while Vella fought for her own self-control. When Matt was near, she couldn't seem to catch her breath and her thoughts were all muddled inside her head. She wanted him with a wildness that frightened her, and although her body begged for his touch, she was terrified of being swept beyond all logic and reason.

Finally she whispered, "Good night, Matt. Thank you for dinner."

Matt struggled to find the words that would send her away from him. "Good night."

He shoved his hands in his pockets so that he wouldn't crush her to him again and kiss her with all the fierce, built-up passion he was feeling. "I'll call you," he added softly. Then he turned on his heel and walked away.

Vella stared after him, her pulse racing, her stomach tied in knots. Would he call? Would she ever see him again? He was leaving, walking rapidly toward his car as if the devil himself were on his heels, as if he couldn't leave fast enough.

"Matt!"

She didn't realize the cry had come from her own lips until it pierced the silence of the dark night.

He half-turned as if he were either unwilling to acknowledge her call, or unsure that he had actually heard it.

They both hovered uncertainly in the pale light, two figures drawn together while they struggled to part.

"Would you like some herbal tea?" Vella ventured at last.

Matt knew he should say no. He couldn't stay here any longer. It was tormenting; she was driving him mad with hunger and desire.

"Yes," he said involuntarily. "Yes, I'd like that." It didn't matter that he didn't like herbal tea. He would stay just a little longer. Just an hour or so more.

"Fine," she said, and he didn't miss the way her smile quivered on her lips.

The short walk back to the porch seemed to take an eternity, even though he bridged the gap in seconds.

When she had unlocked the door, Matt waited for the cat to scurry inside, then followed. Looking around again, he was overcome by a feeling that this was where he belonged. He had never experienced a sensation like it before, and he didn't know what to make of it. Trying to wipe his mind clean of the thought, he told himself that he was being absurd.

"Come into the kitchen," Vella said, turning on lights as she made her way down the hall, consciously avoiding stepping on Sneaky, who scampered at her feet.

What a sight she made, Matt told himself. A magical Indian princess with an adoring cat worshiping at her feet. The sight amused him and a slow smile played on his lips.

He sat down at the table as she put a pot of water on an old-fashioned stove. Her surroundings fitted her so precisely, he thought, gazing around at the decor. In every way, she seemed to live out the many areas of her life that were so unusual, making a different world in each room. Here in the kitchen, the American colonial period was faithfully reproduced, complete with a huge fireplace and black cooking implements.

"Do you take sugar?" she asked as she set cups on the dark wood counter and waited for the kettle to whistle.

He laughed a little. "How about bourbon?"

Vella turned to him in surprise, then smiled. "You don't drink herbal tea," she accused lightly.

He held her eyes. "Not if I can help it. See what I'm willing to do to spend a little more time with you?"

"You should have said so. I'll get you a drink." She prepared her tea, then went with him to the living room.

He sat down on the couch while she mixed a drink, and when she came to him with the glass in

81

one hand and her delicate teacup in the other, he smiled.

"Herbal tea," he said teasingly. "I didn't think anyone really drank that."

Vella grinned at him as she set the beverages on the coffee table and joined him on the couch. "You think I'm eccentric, don't you?" she asked, a playful smile on her lips.

He nodded. "I do, honestly, but that's what's so fascinating about you. I've never met anyone quite like you. I'm not sure I know what to make of it." He caught her hands in his, nodding solemnly. "You are very unusual. Very unusual and very delightful."

Vella attempted to smile, but a vague sense of discomfort rose in her as Debby's words sounded in her ears. She *was* unusual, more unusual than Matt had guessed. Perhaps now was the time to tell him a little more about herself.

She vacillated, wondering how she should begin. She discussed that intimate, secret side of her only with the most special of friends and relatives. Other people knew, too, the people she sometimes helped through crises. But how would she explain it to this man who clearly didn't believe in anything beyond the here and now?

Then suddenly the moment was gone.

Matt pulled her toward him, holding her to his chest as his mouth closed down on hers possessively. The embers that had been smoldering in him all night leaped into full flame, searing his insides as the fire rushed through his blood. He couldn't get enough of Vella. His mouth moved against hers eagerly as his tongue stole inside to taste the moist sweetness.

Vella wrapped her arms around his neck and

drew him more tightly to her, savoring the heady thrill of his caresses, his touch making her forget what had been on her mind seconds earlier. A swift sweetness rose inside her until it blotted out all thoughts of anything but the man in her arms.

His hands were like magic on her skin, heating it until it burned everywhere he touched her. His mouth was an exquisite instrument that coaxed all her passion forth, sending desire spinning through her body. Parting her lips, she met the searching thrusts of his tongue, relishing the rough texture and his delicate probing of the tender inside of her mouth.

Matt's lips trailed down the silken skin of her throat, and Vella arched it so that he would have easy access. She wanted him to touch her everywhere, to feel and caress and explore until she couldn't stand it anymore, until she was borne away to some enchanted place where only he could take her. She had known when he kissed her at the party that he had awakened a desire no other man could ever satisfy.

Matt scattered burning kisses along her skin, and his hands moved over her body restlessly, seeking, yet not satisfied. He wanted to know her as no man ever had before. He wanted to stroke her, to taste her, to become such a part of her that she would never think of love without thinking of him.

He found her lips again and crushed them beneath his, wanting more and more and more. His passion was sweeping him away, taking him somewhere on a tide of love that gained momentum with each touch of her skin. He could be content with nothing less than total surrender from this woman, nothing less than total submission from himself now. His desire was a raging fire, eating up all rational thought. Soon he would be at the mercy of fate.

A ragged groan from his own lips caused him to suddenly draw back from Vella, shaken to the core by his runaway thoughts and passion. When he saw his own desire mirrored in her bright eyes, he reached out to caress the shape of her face. His shaking fingers strayed down her long neck to her breasts to cup them gently.

Vella gazed into his love-darkened eyes, and again she wondered if she should try to make Matt understand about her, about her past, her special ability, before it was too late. But then she realized that it was already too late. She shivered and bowed her head to the inevitable.

But Matt had seen the uncertainty, the hesitation, in her wide gray gaze, and he knew that it echoed his own. Once more he tried to withdraw while there was still the faintest chance left. He knew that he should turn away now, before he tasted all the pleasures that he was sure to find in this woman.

But Vella had already closed her eyes, giving herself up to him. Involuntarily, his hands sought her chignon and he loosened her hair, running shaking fingers through it until it tumbled down her back in dark waves.

His body was burning with desire for her. His mind was calling out to her to love him, to travel to the timeless world of passion and ecstasy. At this moment, it didn't seem that he could go on with his life until he knew her in that elemental melding that only a man and woman can find.

He could exercise control no longer. His mouth moved against hers hungrily, longingly. She was as sensual, as warm, as exciting as he had known she would be. She gave her kisses to him willingly, eagerly, with no restraint. His hands moved down over her body, seeking out each glorious curve. He was on a journey without end, a magical trip that was sure to take him where he had never been before, and he had been in many women's arms. But this one was different. So very different.

As if they had a will of their own, Vella's hands sought out the firm lines of Matt's hard masculine body. Her long fingers traced his chiseled jaw, then stole down his neck to the top button of his shirt, which was open. Stealing inside, she let her fingers stroke the thick hair of his chest, then, wanting to explore more of him, she began to unbutton his shirt. Her lips followed the path of her fingers, and Matt thought he might explode from the effect of her touch.

Fighting a battle for some kind of control, he knew if he claimed Vella he could never walk away from her. She was not a woman a man found satisfaction in and then forgot. In fact, he already knew that he could never forget her, and how much harder it would be if he let her give herself to him.

With a strength and willpower he didn't know he possessed, he eased off her and straightened up on the couch, breathing deeply.

Breathless, stunned by her own unbridled response to him, Vella watched with love-glazed eyes. She told herself that she should thank God that one of them had sense enough to stop while there was still time.

But she hadn't wanted to stop. God forgive her, she had never, never wanted a man so much in her life. It didn't matter that she had known him for only two days. It didn't matter that they were unsuited and without any real hope of a future. She had wanted all of him that he would give. Tonight. Right now.

"I'm sorry," she heard him mutter in a hard, ragged voice. He reached for her hands. "We're going too fast. This is madness."

Although Vella knew the feeling, for he was only echoing her earlier thoughts, she watched him, unable to speak, making no attempt to adjust her disheveled clothing. She was sorry, too, for his hard-earned control could mean nothing else but that he was leaving her.

"I don't usually try to ravish my dates so thoroughly the first time around," he said, trying vainly to inject some humor into the statement.

"It wasn't like that," she murmured. "And I think you know it."

He stood up, clearly still struggling with himself. Without looking at her, he buttoned his shirt.

"I'd better be going now," he said in a husky voice she hardly recognized. Not until he reached the safety of the door did he look back. He stopped in the doorway. For a moment, Vella was sure he would come back to her.

Then he stiffened. "Good-bye, Vella."

"Good-bye, Matt," she all but whispered. She longed to call out to him, but she fought back the desire. When he was ready, she sensed that he would return.

Still, as she watched the door close behind him, she began to tremble. Suddenly tears filled her eyes and began to trickle down her face. She wasn't even quite sure why she was crying; she only knew that in only one day Matt had changed her life. There was an emptiness inside her that she hadn't known existed until he made her aware of it. And now he had gone with no promise of seeing her again.

The tears began to fall faster as she made her way to her bedroom, where she hoped to forget her unhappiness in sleep. But even as she undressed, she knew that there would be no forgetting Matt Colridge. He had always been in her dreams and now that she had touched him, and the dream had somehow become reality, she knew she could never again let him go.

CHAPTER FIVE

Vella awakened with a sense of emptiness she hadn't known since Calan had ceased to be part of her life. She felt again that helpless surge of regret that always accompanied her memories of him. She still felt guilt when she remembered her lost love, though as always, she fought it. She had done her best by Calan; she had tried to get him to listen to her, but he had refused.

Abruptly, she pushed aside the painful thoughts. It had all happened so many years ago. She was only remembering events of the past because of Matt. That thought, too, brought a twinge of regret. She didn't want to consider the possibility that she had lost him, as well.

Tossing back the sheet, she swung her long legs over the side of the bed and brushed the sleep from her eyes. Sneaky stirred more slowly, but by the time Vella had pulled on her housecoat, he was bounding along beside her, ready for breakfast.

As Vella ate her morning meal, she looked longingly at the phone, as if wishing it would ring could make it do so. Her mind still swirling with her dreams of Matt, her body flushing at the memory of the warmth of his fingers, she made herself go upstairs to work. She had four hours before she joined her mother, and the only way she could possibly blot out the maddening memory of the man who had stirred her blood so hotly last night was by working.

She exchanged her nightgown and robe for blue jeans and a white blouse, then tended to her toilet before going to her workroom. She was surprised by the reflection she saw in the bathroom mirror as she washed her face. There was a softness, a glow about her that she had seen only once before —when she had thought she was in love with Calan.

The mere idea of being in love again startled her, and she quickly turned from the mirror. Surely she could not be in love so soon. But then, she had really known Matt all her life. Hadn't his face always appeared before her, teasing her, tempting her to find him? And now she finally had.

Surely they were destined to share their lives. He had to realize that he was meant to be with her. It had been decreed long, long ago, hadn't it? Otherwise, why had his image haunted her for so long?

For the first time in her life, Vella intentionally tried to see what her own future held. She went into the bedroom and seated herself in a chair. Remaining very still and quiet, she meditated, trying to break through today to see if Matt were in her tomorrow. But, as she had suspected she would, she failed. Instinctively, she knew that she could not look at her own future in a quest for happiness. The harder she tried, the more difficult it became.

Eventually she saw thick stands of trees, but she couldn't penetrate them to see beyond, and she didn't know what they symbolized. Was the way eventually to be blocked for her and Matt? Was he already lost to her?

She shook her head, trying to escape the obscure vision. It seemed to take forever to rid herself of the picture, but finally the confines of her own room came back into focus. Eager to free her mind of the turmoil she was experiencing, she went into her study and climbed up on the stool in front of her easel. The sketch of the lilies of the valley stood still and uninspiring before her.

For a long, long time, she sat there, waiting for the total absorption that was necessary for her creative juices to flow. But it never came.

Everywhere she looked, she saw images of Matt, her mind and body whirling with recollections of how he looked and felt. She stared very deliberately at the sketch of the flowers, but Matt's face danced before her eyes, his smiling eyes and laughing lips beckoning to her.

Vella finally gave up on her work. Suddenly she was so eager to talk with her mother that she couldn't wait any longer. She didn't know what she would say or if she would talk about Matt, but the idea of sharing a few hours with the woman who had shaped her life appealed to her immensely.

After running downstairs and picking up her purse, she hurried out to her car. In minutes, she had driven across town to one of the less attractive parts of Palm Springs where apartment houses huddled together, giving shelter to the less affluent and less fortunate.

She shook her head in amazement as she always did when she gazed out at the barren landscapes of the lookalike front yards which skirted the sidewalk. Only one was different—her mother's. Done in a colorful patchwork of multicolored verbena, marigolds, birds-of-paradise, and zinnias, Anne Redding's yard was as cheerful and bright as her personality. As if symbolic of the woman's generous nature, the hardy flowers had long since spilled over into the neighboring yards, spreading their beauty all along the front of the building.

Vella had tried to get Anne to move from here many times, but she would not leave. Any money Vella gave her went to the Indian cause, and any suggestion of living elsewhere was ignored. With a resigned shrug of her shoulders, Vella went up to a first-floor apartment.

She rang the tinny bell many times before her mother finally came to the door. Peering outside with sleepy blue eyes, the woman asked, "Arvella, it isn't noon, is it?"

Vella shook her head. "Nope, I just couldn't wait. I wanted to see you." She glanced down at her watch. "It's eleven."

"Oh."

"Aren't you going to let me in?"

"Oh, yes, of course." Despite the warmth of the day, Anne wrapped a thin Indian shawl around her shoulders, then opened the door wide for her daughter.

Vella smiled to herself as she stepped into the cluttered rooms her mother called home. Everywhere there was evidence of the woman's love for the Indians. There were baskets, sand paintings, and primitive Indian art, and the walls were covered with the handmade quilts her mother prized so highly.

The room fairly throbbed with vibrant colors and life, and oddly enough there was a pleasant sense of harmony in the mating of the Indian decor and the quilts which were a legacy of colonial America.

Vella's eyes skimmed over the paperwork scattered on the coffee table and floor. Anne was forever soliciting one firm or another for help with her various causes, the Indian one being her favorite, and she faithfully replied to each and every source who responded, whether they contributed or not.

There were also stacks of newspapers from all over the country. Her mother believed in the power of the press, and she never missed a chance to make a public plea. Vella knew it all so well, for she had often helped when Anne was in a pinch.

"Why don't you get dressed, Mother?" she said with a fond smile. "I'll stir up something for us to eat."

"You're a good daughter," the woman said, stifling a yawn. "Give me a few minutes, will you?" She grinned a little in embarrassment. "I know I look a sight."

Vella went to the small kitchen–dining room and found a skillet in the cupboard. In minutes, she had concocted cheese omelets and a dish of fresh apple and banana slices. When the toast was brown, she set the food on the table and went to search for her mother.

She met the transformed woman coming down the hall. Again Vella smiled fondly at Anne Redding. Now her mother was in form. Her attire suggested a woman caught between her love for two worlds.

Dressed in a pencil-slim cotton skirt, a white blouse with the collar turned up, an ornate silver belt, moccasins, and a heavy Indian necklace and matching earrings, the fiftyish woman finished tying a red band around one of her gray braids.

"I'm ready, dear."

"Yes, you are," Vella said. "You look great."

She smiled to herself as she followed Anne down the hall. If Matt Colridge thought *she* was eccentric, he should see her mother.

She shook her head at the idea. Poor Matt, senatorial candidate, wouldn't be ready for that.

She felt a bit of sorrow in the knowledge, for her mother was intriguing and unique. She didn't worry much about what other people thought or said; basically she lived to please herself. Vella knew few other people who could do so.

Especially not Matt, she reminded herself; he had the public to answer to. The thought made her shiver inside, and she suppressed it.

"So," Anne said, seating herself across from her daughter. "What brings you here, sweetheart?"

Vella blinked, then told herself that she should have known she couldn't fool her mother. Anne could read her quite well.

"I told you, Mother. I wanted to spend some time with you."

Anne nodded knowingly. "There are some times when you merely want to enjoy my company, but today there's something on your mind."

She picked up her toast and frugally buttered it. When she had spread blackberry jam on it and savored a bite, her clear blue eyes met her daughter's enchanting gray ones. "What's troubling you, Arvella?"

Squirming uncomfortably in her chair, Vella felt like a child again. "What if I told you I think I'm in love?"

"Hallelujah!" her mother cried, tossing down

93

her toast to clap her hands. "And about time! Who's the lucky man?"

"Now, Mother," Vella cautioned, "there's nothing to get so excited about. I've only been out with him once."

Anne Redding's eyes were very calm and serious as they met her daughter's. "A woman loves when her love comes along, Arvella, and you, of all people, would know the right man."

Vella nodded, suddenly feeling shy about telling her mother the details. How could she explain that the same things Anne praised in her—her Indian heritage, her psychic powers, her uniqueness, the things she herself loved best—were the things that Matt would never understand? How could she say that the circumstances of her birth would be bad for Matt's candidacy? She couldn't, of course, and she became quiet.

"And?" Anne prompted eagerly, sensing that there was more.

Vella avoided her mother's eyes. "There's not a lot to say."

"But he's the one, isn't he?" her mother asked. "He's the one, and you're afraid? You can't hide the facts from me, child."

Vella grinned. "No, I suppose not." Her gaze became solemn. "He's the one, Mother, but I don't know if it will work or if it will last." She glanced away, unable to say that she didn't even know if he would see her again. "He's running for senator. You know how I feel about politicians," she added, as if that explained all her fears.

The older woman nodded sagely. "Time will work it out, Arvella. Don't worry love. Let it be free to grow. Time will work it out."

"But, Mother," Vella said with a sudden note of

desperation in her voice, "what if time doesn't? What if I lose him? Considering the circumstances, wouldn't it be easier not to take the chance?"

"Absolutely not," Anne said with conviction. Her voice softened and her eyes became misty. "I did lose your father, but, oh, Arvella, the hours I spent with him were worth more than any treasure on earth. I wouldn't trade that time for my own life."

Vella nodded, and she knew in that instant what her mother was talking about. Even if she never had another moment with Matt, her life was richer for having met him and known his touch. But she wanted more. So much more.

As though both women sensed that they had agreed on the crucial point, they began to talk about other things. The hours sped by, and before either woman was ready to relinquish their special time together, the doorbell rang.

"My ladies," Anne whispered. "They must be early."

Vella looked at her watch and shook her head. "No. They're right on time." She stood up as her mother did.

"Won't you stay and join us?"

Vella declined. "I really must get back to work."

The two women embraced for a long moment. "Be happy, Arvella," Anne said softly. "We're here in this particular moment of time so briefly." Her sparkling blue eyes met her daughter's solemn gray gaze. "Be yourself and accept life," she added gently. "Don't fight it so hard."

Vella felt as if her mother had looked straight into her heart and seen the turbulence there. The two women stared at each other for a moment,

95

then Vella nodded. Arm in arm, they walked to the door. When Vella had been introduced to the women, she smiled at her mother once more, then left.

The phone was ringing as Vella walked up to her front door. With eager fingers, she turned the key in the lock and hurried inside. She felt the excited beating of her heart as she raced across the floor. Praying that it was Matt on the line, she snatched up the receiver.

"Hello," she said breathlessly.

"Vella, I've been trying to get you for hours," Debby cried. "I've been waiting for you to call and let me know how your date with Matt went."

Attempting not to let her friend know how disappointed she was that the caller wasn't Matt, Vella replied, "I've been at Mother's."

"So, how was your date?"

Vella laughed. Debby had never been one easily distracted from her main course. "It was wonderful," she answered honestly, her voice taking on a dreamy tone. "He's an incredible man."

"Where did you go? Did he make a play for you?"

"Debby!" Vella cried in exasperation. "You really go right for the intimate details."

"Yes," her friend said bluntly, "and I'm dying to hear them. Do you know that half the socialites in this town have their hearts set on Matthew Colridge? He's the hit of the season. Why, I've had women calling me on the phone trying to get me to arrange another meeting with him."

Vella's own heart sank. Any one of those women would be so much better suited to Matt than she.

She couldn't resist asking the question on her mind.

"Do you know if he has a special woman? I suspect that's where he went so late the night of your party."

"I think he had some kind of political meeting," Debby said. "You really are interested in him, aren't you?"

"Just curious, I think," Vella hedged, then, as vaguely as possible, she went over the details of her date with him.

"And did you tell him about—you know—about your extrasensitivity?" Debby asked.

Vella silently shook her head. No, she hadn't told him. She didn't know how to.

"Vella?"

"No," she replied honestly. "I meant to, but I didn't get around to it."

"Oh, dear," Debby said in a somewhat worried tone. "Vella, you really must tell him before this gets out of hand. For goodness sake, he's an ex-military man, a man running for a high political office. The longer you procrastinate, the harder it will be. I don't need to remind you of how Calan felt, do I? And you can't keep such a thing a secret."

"It doesn't matter," Vella interjected. "He didn't ask me out again."

There was a brief pause before Debby spoke. "What went wrong?"

Vella sighed unhappily. "I think we both realized the futility of continuing this thing," she said. But it was a lie. Maybe Matt had realized that, but she hadn't realized it at all, and the mere thought caused her to sink into a depression.

"Maybe he'll call you again. If not, perhaps it's all for the best," Debby said.

"Listen, Deb," Vella said abruptly, "I really would love to chat, but my visit with Mother threw me off schedule, and I've got to run." She couldn't bear to talk any longer about Matt.

"Gee, I was hoping we could get together," Debby said. "Are you behind schedule? I thought you had finished your card."

"I've already received the verse for another. That's how I earn my living, you know," Vella said in a teasing voice she had to force herself to use. "If I don't chain myself to the stool and easel, I don't eat."

Debby laughed because both women knew it wasn't quite the truth, yet it wasn't a lie either. Vella was very successful, but she wouldn't stay on top for long if she didn't stick to self-imposed schedules.

"All right, but you be sure and give me a call later in the week. Promise?"

"Promise. Bye, Deb."

With a weary sigh, Vella replaced the phone, then curled up in a chair nearby. Why was she punishing herself like this? Jumping each time the phone rang, praying that it would be Matt?

Feeling despondent, she wandered back to the kitchen and prepared an early supper. Then she took a long bath, found a favorite book, and went to bed early. When sleep finally came, her dreams were a replay of the night before. With Matt heavy on her mind, she tossed and turned through the night.

The next morning Vella went immediately from the breakfast table to her studio, determined to work. Still, it was a mighty struggle; for the first few minutes, she kept remembering Matt as she had seen him—first on her Indian card, then here in her room. Gradually, she used her thoughts of him to set the theme for her painting.

Settling into a pensive mood, she lost herself deeper and deeper in the project, the way she preferred to work. She liked to be so submerged in the subject that the real world ceased to exist for her.

Eventually, she found the Indian motif that was always a part of her work. The picture of the lilies of the valley slowly, subtly evolved into the lovely face of an Indian girl: small, individual flowers began to form the faint image of eyes, nose, mouth, and lips. Other flowers were positioned so that the petals shaped a head, the stems coming together to outline a slender, delicate neck.

For a brief moment, the image of her own face flashed across the imaginary woman's, and Vella recognized in an instant the look of love she had seen when she'd looked in the mirror earlier. She was creating a lover for the Indian man who now lived on forever on her last greeting card. She smiled again, liking the idea of matching up two lovers who could never be touched by time or tragedy.

Now that she had the premise, she began to work more easily, painstakingly making the magic that was hers alone to create. She let her mind go, for the first time allowing any and all thoughts of Matt to flow freely as she created the woman who would be the mate to the Indian man.

She made the woman as beautiful and wondrous as she herself would like to be for Matt, and, always, she was aware of the glow of love that graced the dark eyes and Mona Lisa mouth of the lovely creature emerging under her skilled fingers.

Untouched by the complications and uncertainties of life, the maiden gradually formed, the secrets of time and love subtly written across her dark features, which surfaced so magically and mysteriously on the fragile petals of the lilies of the valley.

Engrossed in her work, Vella lost all thought of time as she worked on through the hours, a definite goal now in mind. She knew the work was good, for it was coming from her heart, and she was ever conscious of the new heightened awareness of pleasure Matt had created inside her. It gave her work a sparkle, a dimension which it had never quite had before.

When the phone rang unexpectedly, Vella cried out in surprise. She had so totally abandoned herself to the thoughts of Matt that she subconsciously imagined that he was the caller.

"Hello." The breathless anticipation was evident in her voice.

"Hello, Pretty. It's Dwayne."

Abruptly catapulted into the real world, Vella shook herself free of the magic she had created. "Dwayne, how are you?"

She was so disappointed that tears rushed to her eyes as she glanced at the clock. It was after six. An entire day had gone by in which she had lived with the memory of Matt, but it had all been fantasy.

This was the real world, a world of Dwaynes and Debbies reminding her that she had not heard a single word from Matt in two days—and reminding her that perhaps never again would she know the touch of his mouth and hands stirring her so pleasurably. She could create all the imaginary characters she wanted, matchmake forever in her paintings, but where was Matt?

"How about going out to dinner with me this week?"

The persuasive sound of Dwayne's well-modulated voice brought Vella sharply back to reality. She forced a little warmth into her voice. "How thoughtful of you to ask, Dwayne. I appreciate it, but I'm afraid I'm going to be too busy all week to do much socializing. You know how it is with us self-employed people."

There was disappointment in his voice when he spoke again. "Can't you take off one evening for dinner? I'm self-employed, too, but I do manage to eat on occasion."

"I'm sorry," she said politely, "but I really can't take the time." She sighed softly. "I enjoyed seeing you at Debby's, Dwayne. I hope we'll see each other again on such occasions in the future." There was no point in encouraging him when Matt was the only man she could think of.

Dwayne understood that Vella was telling him there was no point in persisting. "I hope so, Vella. I enjoy your company."

"Thank you. Good night."

When she had hung up, Vella sat for a long time, staring at the phone, wondering if she would ever hear from Matt again. Two days wasn't so long, after all, but the way he had left, without any promise for the future, made her afraid to hope. And yet, how could she do otherwise?

Knowing the only way to save her sanity was to keep busy, she went downstairs to make dinner. Sneaky, hearing his mistress, came bounding in through the cat door to share in the meal. Then,

101

for the second night, Vella went to bed early, feeling very much alone.

She was up earlier than usual the next morning. Eager to concentrate on her painting of the Indian woman, she tossed on jeans, a shirt, and slippers, and went down for a cup of coffee. Today she had no time for breakfast. Sometime in the night, in the heart of her dreams, she had found further inspiration for her painting.

Hastening through her morning routine, she was soon settled on her tall stool, intent on her project. When the phone rang before nine, she glanced at it askance, vaguely irritated by the interruption. This time she wasn't foolish enough to think it would be Matt. Wishing, as she sometimes did, that she had an answering machine, she impatiently reached for the receiver.

"Hello."

"Vella, Matt here."

Her heart began to pound wildly. The mere sound of his voice was enough to give wings to her soul and stir her from all the practical thoughts she had tried to concentrate on in the past few days.

"How are you?" she asked, trying to sound calm.

"Mad about you."

Vella could feel her pulse pound at her temples. "Oh?" was all she could manage to say as she waited for him to continue.

"I've tried to give myself some time to cool off, to be reasonable and rational where you're concerned," he said, "but, lady, I'm hopelessly crazy about you. Would I be imposing, disturbing your schedule too much if I asked you to spend the day with me?"

When Vella was too caught off guard to respond, Matt paused, then continued. "I know it's short notice again, but I hoped you'd want to go up on the tram with me today." Vella heard the laughter in his voice. "Don't disappoint me. I've already made a lunch—of sorts," he added.

"I'd like that," she told him. She hadn't been up to Mount San Jacinto in some time, and she had always enjoyed the spectacular views. Once she had used the mountainside for the background of a card. But the lure of the mountain scenery wasn't what tempted her. Anywhere with Matt would sound appealing.

"Good. Shall I pick you up in an hour?"

"Fine."

Vella still held the phone to her ear after Matt had hung up. For a few minutes, she recalled each word of the brief conversation, then suddenly she sprang from the stool. An hour he had said. She had to get ready.

She rushed to her room. Glancing in the mirror, she bemoaned the sight of her hair. She looked so helter-skelter today, and she could do nothing with the thick masses of black on such short notice. Suddenly the image of her mother in braids flashed into her mind, and she decided that she, too, would wear braids, but she would weave the two together with ribbon.

Rummaging around in her closet, she finally decided on blue jeans with a faint white stripe in them, and a long-sleeved blouse, because she knew it would be cool up around the summit.

After a quick shower, she dressed in her outfit and tennis shoes, then plaited her hair. Her fingers were trembling as she finished dressing and studied herself in the mirror. The effect wasn't quite what she wanted; still, she reminded herself, she was only going on a picnic.

But she was going with Matt, her heart told her. And once again, she felt the excited beating as she went downstairs to await his arrival.

The only thought that surfaced to dampen her exuberance was the fact that now she knew she must tell him about her extrasensitivity. She couldn't put it off any longer. Debby was right about that, and well she knew it. But she didn't relish the idea at all. She was very much afraid that the conversation would bring about the end of her dreams.

CHAPTER SIX

When Matt arrived, Vella opened the door to find him dressed in blue jeans that outlined his long, muscular legs and narrow hips, and a V-necked navy blue sweater that molded to his broad shoulders. He was potently masculine, and Vella's eyes strayed to the hair curling out darkly over the V of the sweater. Abruptly, she remembered how crisp Matt's chest hair had felt to her sensitive fingertips and she blushed lightly.

"May I come in?"

She glanced back up at his teasing blue eyes. "Yes, of course. Excuse my impoliteness."

He laughed. "I'd like to think you were bowled over by my appearance. I know the sight of you made me forget everything—for a moment."

Vella smiled at his teasing tone, but she knew the compliment was sincere.

She stepped back for him to enter, and when she had closed the door, he turned suddenly and pulled her into his arms.

"Vella, Vella," he murmured thickly, holding her to his hard body, "it's so good to see you again. I can't seem to think of anything but you day and night."

His breath was warm on her ear and Vella trembled at the emotion in his voice. She wanted to tell him she felt the same, too, but something held her back. She had been too willing, too forward with him the last time. She would have to be patient and let him take his time with her.

"I'm glad," she whispered, trying to keep the tremor from her voice.

He held her away a little to gaze deeply into her eyes, then lowered his head and touched her mouth with his. At first the kiss was tender and exploratory, but suddenly Matt hugged Vella's body to his, groaning hungrily as he tasted her lips.

It wasn't what he had intended. When he made plans to see her today, he had promised himself that he would court her leisurely, but now he found that very difficult, if not impossible. He felt as if he had been away from her for weeks, months, forever. Abruptly, he held her at arm's length again.

She confused him, swamped his senses, wove a magic web around him that blinded him to anything but her. When he was near her, he couldn't think rationally; she somehow caught him in her spell, making him irresponsible and foolish. Today he felt the same way he had on the night he met her. She had a strange, indefinable power over him that he couldn't seem to escape.

He honestly couldn't understand what was happening to him. He was a methodical man, a man who planned and scheduled the events in his life. Those traits had made him a good soldier, a good leader—and they would make him a good senator.

But with Vella all his best intentions became muddled and distorted. Could this be the thing they called love, he asked himself? Was he fighting against himself in a battle already lost? As a good soldier, he knew when to attack and when to retreat. Shouldn't he now know when to surrender?

For two days he had forced himself to stay away from Vella so that he could regain his equilibrium and stop behaving like a love-crazy teenager. Yet the moment he looked into her enchanting gray eyes, he was lost again.

"I'm sorry," he murmured huskily. "I hadn't meant to do that." He looked around the room. "Do you have a sweater or jacket? It'll be cool up on the mountain, I'm told, and if we don't get going, I'm afraid I'm going to make love to you right here and now."

Vella *wanted* Matt Colridge to make love to her. It was all she had thought about since he held her in his arms on the couch in this very room three long nights ago. But she knew he was right; this was not the time to lose themselves completely in each other.

"Yes," she said, taking a blue cape from a coat rack.

"That's very smart," Matt commented, looking at the unique garment and trying desperately to keep his mind on neutral subjects.

"Thank you," she said.

He smiled at her as she started toward the door. He couldn't seem to stop staring at her. His eyes roved over her braid and he wanted to trace the dark woven texture with his fingertips. The very simplicity of the style made it all the more beautiful.

When they had settled in his car, Vella glanced into the back seat at the picnic basket and blanket. "We really are going on a picnic, aren't we?" she asked, a twinkle in her gray eyes. "I haven't done that since I was a child."

107

He grinned at her as he smoothly started the car. "In some ways I think you're *still* a child—a beautiful and fascinating one."

Vella could feel her cheeks flush at the compliment. "We should all keep some of the child alive in us," she said.

Matt reached out to squeeze her hand. "I agree completely."

The words were easy to say, but he knew the child in him had died in the agonies of war. Maybe that was part of what attracted him to Vella, he thought. She was unlike anyone he had ever known. There was a magic, a wonder, about her that made her what she was, and he realized that he admired her immensely. Not only was she rare and beautiful, but she also had sensitivity and depth.

They drove to the tram in silence, both of them seeming unable to believe that they were together again. Vella felt her excitement escalate as they approached the parking area for the trip up the mountain.

"Have you gone up before?" she asked.

He shook his head. "I told you I was going to rely on you to show me the sights."

She laughed. "It'll be my pleasure."

When he had parked the car, he helped Vella out, then handed her the blanket. Picnic basket in one hand and her hand in the other, they walked to the ticket station.

In minutes, they joined many other passengers for the spectacular climb from the parched desert sands of Palm Springs to the pines of Mount San Jacinto State Park. The eighty-passenger cable car was soon packed to capacity, but Matt had managed to find a spot for Vella and himself at the back so they could look out over the Coachella Valley below.

Standing closely behind her with his arms around her waist, the picnic basket and folded blanket between his feet, Matt protected Vella from the jostling of the other excited riders, all exclaiming about the view from the glass windows.

"It's beautiful, isn't it?" Matt murmured, gazing past Vella as the car began its assent to the 8,516-foot level of the mountain.

"Yes," she said, but she wasn't even aware of the splendid panorama of the desert below or the changing scenery of the mountainsides.

Suddenly, there was nothing in her world but Matt. Experiencing a feeling of *déjà vu,* she recalled the moment just before she had met him at Debby's party. She had had a vision in which she and a man were suspended somewhere in midair, and she had had a sensation of height, splendor, and incredible excitement.

Now, in the cocoon of Matt's arms, she felt as if she had been borne away by a mythical bird with silver wings, sheltered in a secret world that included only Matt and her. The chatter of the other passengers faded away and she knew only the wonder of the man standing so near, the heat of his powerful body almost touching hers, the strength of his arms as they molded around her protectively to grasp the bar in front of her, keeping them both steady in the rising cable car.

In a flash, she realized that this was her vision, this single moment when reality fell away along with the ground beneath. Surely, it was yet another sign that they had a future, that they were destined to be together.

When the car lurched to a stop inside the mountain station, Vella was shaken from her memories. Unprepared for the abrupt cessation of movement, she was thrown heavily against Matt's right arm.

Clasping his arms tightly around her waist to steady her, he murmured, "Are you all right?"

Vella glanced back over her shoulder. "Yes. I'm fine." And she was, except for the rush of fire that raced over her skin at the touch of Matt's hands on her body.

He took her hand again as the others began to disembark, and she walked with him into the mountain lodge, trying her best to keep her mind on something besides his magnetic appeal.

"Which way to the trails and picnic facilities?" he asked, his blue eyes bright as he looked at her.

Vella led him through the building, which housed shops and a restaurant, to an outside door. "This way," she said. "Pick your direction. There are fifty-four miles of hiking trails."

Matt grinned as he looked up at the towering trees. "This is nice. The desert has its own beauty, but this is very refreshing."

Vella agreed fully, as she followed him down a pathway he had chosen at random.

"Let's sneak away from the others," he told her, winking playfully. "I want you all to myself." His eyes met hers for a moment, and he was suddenly very serious. "I can't begin to tell you how I've missed you, Vella. It seems like I've looked for you my whole life, and the two days we've been apart have been an eternity for me."

He truly hadn't meant to confess that just yet, but now that the words were out, he sighed in resignation. Somewhere between the desert

110

ground below and the tall mountain pines, he had lost his footing completely and had been totally captivated by Vella's charms. Even he, the adamant strategist, knew there was no point in waging a war against the feelings he had for this woman.

Shivering, Vella fought back a sudden desire to tell him that she had seen his face for years, that she had looked for him her whole life. It wasn't the time yet; she needed to pick just the right moment and the right words, but there was no denying that she had to talk to him. As she looked into his eyes, she promised herself that she would do so before they went down the mountain to the valley again.

Matt suddenly felt very carefree; it was as if his admission of his love for Vella had released him from his mental turmoil. He began to relax once more, for he was confident that they could somehow work out any differences they had.

After all, when he had succumbed to what he thought was love before, he had been only eighteen. He could handle the experience now. They would talk it all out; discussion was the key to communication and understanding. But there would be plenty of time for that later. Now was the time for letting their relationship take its natural course. He was in a jovial mood as they worked their way deeper into the woods, admiring the scenery.

Vella laughed along with him as he talked about his past as a Boy Scout. He was charming and entertaining, and it didn't take her long to forget that she had promised herself she would talk about her own past. She was eager to hear all about him, and she let his words flow over her like music.

When they found an isolated spot, hidden in the

tall pines, they agreed that it was the ideal place for a picnic. Matt set the basket down, and he and Vella spread the blanket out over the soft pine needles. The spot was so secluded that they couldn't easily be seen from the trail.

"Maybe we shouldn't have chosen this area," Matt said, his eyes glowing brightly. "Without the public to act as my watchdog, I don't know if I can keep my hands off you."

Vella laughed, but Matt knew he was only half joking. As he gazed at the tall, dark beauty, he wanted nothing more than to hold her to his body again and know the pleasure of tracing her curves with his hands. He had dreamed of her relentlessly, been tormented by his thoughts of her, until he knew he had to have her. Now that the fight with his doubts was over, he wanted only to surrender to the pulsing desire that battered at his senses, calling out so urgently to him.

Vella settled down on the blanket, stretching her long, slim legs out before her, and Matt sat down nearby. Trying to keep his hands occupied so that he didn't ache to touch her, he opened the basket and began to take out the contents.

Vella could hardly hold back her laughter as he laid before them peanut butter sandwiches, apples, wine, and the most wretched-looking cake she had ever seen.

"My heavens! Who was the cook?" she asked, laughter in her voice.

Matt grinned at her. "Now, don't make fun. I prepared this exquisite fare myself. Right down to the cake." He laughed. "I want you to sample the kinds of things I have to pretend to enjoy on the campaign trail. Good down-home cooking, we call it."

Vella laughed. "Surely you haven't been fed peanut butter sandwiches?"

"I have. I kid you not," he insisted. "Anyway, I kept in mind that you're a vegetarian."

Vella giggled with delight. "Honestly, there's plenty of selection for a vegetarian without resorting to peanut butter," she said, but nevertheless she loved his picnic meal.

And she admired Matt. He had a great sense of humor, and she couldn't recall the last time she had had so much fun with a man. He had an easy, ready wit, which she suspected had been honed by speech-making and campaigning. Here in the woods he seemed much more relaxed than she had ever seen him. She attributed it to his break from politicking, and she was happy to see him so playful.

As they ate the gooey sandwiches and washed them down with expensive white wine served in plastic cups, Vella laughed at the stories he told her about the campaign trail. When he held up the miserable, collapsed cake and insisted that he had diligently followed the recipe one of the voters had given him, she dissolved into laughter.

"You couldn't have followed the directions," she insisted, unable to stop laughing. "That's the worst-looking thing I've seen recently."

"But I did," he contended, merriment making his blue eyes dance. "You'll hurt my feelings if you don't try it."

Vella couldn't believe he was serious, but she went along with him. However, when they sampled the cake after the wine, it was worse than it looked. The rich chocolate icing was overpowering after the tart drink, and Vella couldn't eat it, no

113

matter who had made it. Laughing, she refused to have more than a single taste.

Matt grabbed for her, pretending to force her to have a second bite, but abruptly he dropped the piece of cake and pulled Vella into his arms. He knew of nothing sweeter than the taste of her, and he couldn't resist a single kiss. His lips smothered her laughter, and Vella wrapped her arms around his neck, wanting to draw him even closer.

Stretching out over her, Matt lightly rested his weight on her body, and Vella was aware of every hard line of him, from his broad chest to his muscled thighs. She felt the quickening of her desire, and she eagerly returned the hard, demanding kisses Matt gave her.

When his tongue slipped into her mouth to stroke hers, she met it with her own. Her body responded primitively and automatically to his, her hips moving ever so slightly.

"Oh, Matt," she murmured, "Matt."

Suddenly a bold squirrel chattered nearby, eager for some of the abandoned cake, and Vella and Matt pulled apart in surprise. As they looked at each other, they didn't know whether to laugh or to be embarrassed.

"Good Lord, woman," Matt muttered low. "I was so hungry for you that I forgot we're in the woods of a state park." He tried to force a smile to his lips. "I can just see the caption on the picture in a newspaper now: *Senatorial Candidate Caught Seducing Beauty in Woods While Boy Scouts Watch.*"

Vella tried to laugh, but she had been abruptly reminded of things she needed to say. Now, while the moment was at hand, she had to get it over with.

"Matt—" she began, but he interrupted her.

"Nope. Don't try to lure me back into your arms," he teased. "We'd better go while we still can."

He looked up at her with a smile in his eyes. On his knees, he was already gathering up the picnic supplies. "And don't feel too bad because we didn't eat the cake. I didn't really make it. One of the women I met at your friend Debby's house brought it to me at eight o'clock this morning, explaining that her thirteen-year-old daughter had made it."

He smiled. "I don't know if I believe her story about the daughter, but I accepted the cake with gratitude. It gave me the idea for this picnic with you."

Vella shook her head, but the moment for revealing herself to him had passed. She couldn't bear to dampen the marvelous mood. They were leaving. She would talk to Matt when they returned to her house.

His good humor was high as they worked their way back through the trees to the station to make the trip down on the tram. While they waited, they gazed out the windows of the building at the stunning view below, and Vella suppressed thoughts of the inevitable conversation she must have with Matt. He made her forget that there was anything in the world worth worrying about when she was with him.

It had been such a carefree and idyllic day that her fears seemed exaggerated and foolish. She suspected that he cared deeply for her, as she did for him. Her mother was right. It was best not to worry love. There was still plenty of time. But the nagging doubts stayed at the corners of her mind, because Matt didn't really know her at all.

Both Matt and Vella were thoughtful as they made the journey back to her house. Matt knew it was time to talk to her about her role in his life and his career. Absurd as it seemed, sometime during the day he had made up his mind that he was going to have this woman for his wife.

Only the particulars were left to be decided upon. He had promised himself that he would never again attempt to change someone else, and he meant to stand by that. But he had to have Vella for his own.

All at once he couldn't imagine life without her. He didn't want to court her any longer, to follow formalities, to delay their life together. Surely they could make a relationship work, in spite of their differences. After all, hadn't someone smarter than he said that love conquered all?

When Vella looked at him questioningly, he grinned. "I hope you don't have any plans for tonight. I know the picnic lunch wasn't much, and I want to take you somewhere really special for dinner. Are you free?"

Vella didn't tell him that she would have broken a thousand dates for him. "You really do like to do everything on the spur of the moment, don't you?" she asked teasingly.

"Don't say you've got another date," he said, his eyes darkening. He couldn't stand to think of her with another man.

She smiled. "I'm free."

He seemed tremendously relieved. "Good," he said, then he became pensive as his gaze returned to the road. When he stopped in front of Vella's house, he pulled her over to him for the briefest of kisses, then released her.

"Get dressed in your finest," he told her as he gently stroked her left hand. "Tonight we're going to have a dinner to remember. Can you be ready by seven?"

Vella nodded, even though she hated to see him leave again.

"Good. I'll be back with bells on."

She laughed at the clichéd expression, then slid from the car. She watched as he waved, then drove off. Although she hated to see him go, she could feel the excitement building inside her as never before. She couldn't shake the feeling that tonight was going to change her life. She wasn't quite sure why or how, but the feeling would not leave her.

Her entire body surging with excitement, she raced up to the door and let herself inside. Sneaky bounded up from nowhere, but she hardly noticed him. She had to find something extra special to wear, something that would add to the memory of this evening, for she had no doubt that it would be very memorable indeed.

As Matt drove through the downtown area en route to his home, he realized that for the first time in years, he was letting his emotions guide him. He'd thought himself incapable of such abandon, but Vella had shown him things he never knew about himself before.

He glanced idly into a jewelry store as he waited for a red light, and his gaze fell on a silver pin fashioned like a magic wand; the star-shaped head featured a single glittering diamond and the rod was studded with tiny stones. Matt was reminded

117

of the spell Vella had cast on him, and impulsively he decided that he had to have the wand for her.

It was a frivolous thing, and he wasn't usually given to such spur-of-the-moment purchases, but it seemed in keeping with his recent behavior. Maybe this was the way love was meant to be: impulsive, reckless, and crazy. He felt precisely that way about Vella, as if he were being swept away on a magic carpet to some incredibly enchanting land where conventional rules didn't apply.

Time was running short by the time he located a parking place and purchased the pin. While he was waiting for it to be gift wrapped, he found himself glancing at the engagement rings.

"Will there be something else, sir?" the clerk asked politely.

Matt's eyes strayed to the rings again, and he mentally shook his head. The ring he selected for Vella would take much thought, for he wanted it to be as special as the woman who would wear it. He would not shop for it in haste.

"May I use the phone to make a local call?" he asked, determined to distract himself from even the thought of buying Vella a diamond ring now.

When the clerk consented, Matt made reservations at an exclusive restaurant. He didn't believe in using his status for special attention, but this was one time he was pleased when he was told that a table could certainly be found for him. There were certain advantages to being well-known.

Despite the fact that there were only a couple of hours before Matt would pick her up for dinner, Vella found herself wound up and restless as she went up to her bedroom to select something ap-

118

propriate for the evening. Her gaze wandered distractedly over her dresses, her mind on Matt.

Abruptly she decided that she had to get out of the house for a little while. She needed to expend some of the nervous energy she was feeling before Matt came for her. She was as flighty as a wild bird, and that wasn't at all like her. When she returned, perhaps she would have a better idea of what she wanted to wear, but her mood was so erratic that she couldn't decide now.

She found herself driving aimlessly through the crowded downtown streets, unable to focus on anything definite. Such behavior wasn't at all like her, but then she hadn't been herself since she had met Matt.

Suddenly she saw a beautiful outfit in a store window, and she knew in an instant that she *had* to have the dress and shoes for tonight. She was a little surprised at herself, for although she enjoyed clothes, she had never been one to buy impulsively. The shop was one of Palm Springs's more exclusive ones, and the outfit was sure to cost a fortune.

Besides, she didn't even know if she could get the dress in her size. She only knew that she wanted it fervently. Her intuition had already told her that this was going to be a very special night, and she wanted to look beautiful for Matt.

With a mixture of anticipation and anxiety, she hunted for a place to park. Eventually she pulled into a lot on a side street and walked back to the shop.

The dress was one of a kind, and, fortunately Vella's size. When the clerk took it from the window, Vella gasped at the price tag, but she was not discouraged.

The silver-colored dress, accented by bands of blue and gold ribbons around the neckline, sleeves, and hem, was more beautiful than Vella had first thought. It had a magical quality and the silky texture felt good to her sensitive fingers. She knew it was right for her and this evening.

For once, she was going by her instincts where Matt was concerned, as her mother had bid her. When she tried the dress on, she realized that she welcomed the idea of being frivolous for a change. She was eager to lose some of her hard-fought-for control and seize the moment with Matt. She had always been able to advise others to live for the here and now and to trust their feelings, but she had never learned how to apply that to her own life—until Matt.

She realized that she wanted him with all her heart, forever, and somewhere, in the back of her mind, she soothed her fears, telling herself that love could indeed conquer anything. After all, if fate had decreed that she and Matt become as one, surely her past and present couldn't change that.

The lovely garment scooped low in a heart shape across Vella's shoulders and bosom, to be tied at the form-fitting waist by ribbons in blue, gold, and silver, then flared into a full scalloped skirt which swirled rhythmically about her long legs when she turned. The clerk exclaimed over her beauty as Vella modeled the dress, and she hoped it would have the same effect on Matt.

Vella felt that it was all meant to be when the high-heeled silver shoes which complemented the dress fit perfectly. She could hardly wait until the clerk had boxed the outfit, and when she had signed the charge slip, she hurried back to her car like a young girl with special prizes.

120

She drove home in a fog, trying her best to remain calm when she thought about the coming evening. Only Matt had the power to send her senses and expectations reeling until she couldn't think logically. When she had entered the house, she told herself that what she needed was a long soak in the tub to get her thoughts in order and stop behaving like an excited schoolgirl.

The relaxing bath did the trick, and when she emerged from the warm, soapy water half an hour later, she was once again in control, although she realized that nothing could quell her burning eagerness to see Matt.

He himself had said this was going to be a special night, and though she tried not to let her imagination run away with her, she couldn't deny the fact that she felt Matt was destined to be hers. Would tonight be the night that proved it? She didn't know, but her heart kept whispering that it would be.

CHAPTER SEVEN

By the time Matt rang the doorbell, Vella was dressed in the gorgeous silver outfit, her hair left to flow loosely down her back in shimmering black waves made by the braid she had worn earlier in the day.

Matt was dressed in a rich blue suit and a darker blue-and-white-striped shirt which accented his magnificent eyes. Tonight they seemed bluer than ever, and Vella felt the now familiar heightened awareness at the sight of him.

For a moment, Matt simply stared at her, his blue eyes blazing. She was the most exquisite vision he had ever seen, and he could hardly believe he had found her at last. Standing there in that dress, smiling softly at him, her gray eyes more mysterious than ever, she was the answer to all his dreams, the silver lining in his cloud.

"You're too beautiful to be real," he murmured, letting his gaze rove over her. Then, suddenly, he was impatient to get on with the evening. He felt as though he were about to ignite and a single touch of this woman's hand would send him into orbit.

"Are you ready? I've made reservations for seven-thirty."

"Yes," she said, unable to deny the savage

pounding of the pulse at her temples. She turned back to the couch for a tiny silver clutch bag and Matt took the opportunity to let his eyes feast on her loveliness.

The restaurant he had chosen was along Restaurant Row in Rancho Mirage and, as he assisted Vella from the car, leaving it for the valet to park, he asked, "Have you eaten here?"

She shook her head as she looked at the elaborate Italian villa. "No, I haven't yet had the pleasure, but I've been told it's not to be missed."

"I hope you won't be disappointed," he said, taking her hand to lead her inside.

There was no way she could have been. Decorated in 1920s Italian style, the restaurant was exotic and exciting with its vibrant colors and authentic paintings. Intimate tables with muted light from many candles accented single red roses in cut glass vases, stiff white napkins against ruby tablecloths, and fine china and silver place settings.

Vella and Matt were shown to a table for two, hidden in the midst of lush greenery. A small waterfall gurgled enchantingly nearby. A musical quartet sequestered somewhere in an alcove sang Italian love songs in soft, crooning voices.

"This is wonderful," Vella murmured, her eyes glowing as she looked across the table at Matt. If she weren't already in love, this would certainly be the perfect setting to let herself fall, she thought.

"I want it to be an evening you'll remember," he told her huskily. There was so much more he wanted to say to her, but he was determined that he wouldn't rush things. He wanted just the right moment to tell her that he loved her. He was so much in love that he ached for her, but he wouldn't deprive either of them of this slow and magic memory.

When a waiter appeared, Matt ordered a very expensive French wine. Then they selected manicotti and scaloppine al funghi from the menu.

The wine was served in exquisite crystal goblets, and Matt held his up. "To us, Vella, and to this evening."

When she touched her glass to his, he suddenly looped his arm around hers and leaned over so that he could sip from her glass. Her eyes sparkling, Vella took a sip from his.

The food was delicious, and the conversation, against the background of the Italian quartet, seemed unusually romantic. There was no talk of careers or backgrounds, only dreams and hopes and ideals. Vella was once again reminded of how idealistic Matt was, and she found it easy enough to avoid any unpleasant topics.

After they leisurely ate a dessert of cannoli, Vella fully expected Matt to take her home, but he clasped her hand warmly in his and led her into the cocktail lounge, where the quartet was still playing. The couple settled into a small booth and ordered cappuccino. Then Matt guided Vella out onto the dance floor.

Holding her close, he moved with her to the gentle strains of the Italian violins. The wine had mellowed Vella, and she was easily lured by the magic of Matt's touch. Sighing contentedly, she locked her fingers behind his neck. Her eyes meeting his, she smiled.

He lowered his head and gently touched her lips, then cupped her neck so that her head rested on his shoulder. There were other dancers on the floor, but Vella wasn't aware of them. He was all that existed for her as they swayed dreamily to the music, their bodies touching so intimately that she could hear Matt's heart echo the beat of her own. As he had intended, he had made this a most memorable night for her. It would live on in her dreams, no matter what course their relationship took from now on.

When the song ended, Matt still held Vella, waiting for the music to begin again. When it did, the Italians unexpectedly began to sing in perfect English.

The familiar, unforgettable lyrics of a classic love song drifted over Vella, echoing the thoughts in her own head. The words spoke of undying love and the promise of the future.

"Vella."

The gentle sound of her name on Matt's lips caused Vella to look up into his eyes.

"I love you, Vella."

Her heart immediately took up its erratic beat. This was what she had dreamed of, prayed for, and, briefly, she gloried in the sweet sound of Matt's words.

But only briefly, for the reality of his love was bittersweet. It was too soon for such confessions. There was still the matter of who and what each of them was; Vella had forgotten the differences between them because she had wanted to.

"Matt," she began, the magic of the evening evaporating in a single moment. "You don't really know me."

"I know enough," he whispered. "I know that I love you."

But Vella wasn't so sure. She had desperately wanted to hear him say those words, but now, with the whisper of their meaning hovering before her, she felt the full knowledge of all the differences between them like a discordant note that destroyed the harmony of a perfect piece.

"Matt, I really think we're moving much too fast. There are things that must be—"

"Shh," he murmured. "I know it's sudden, but I feel it's right. I love you. I want to make you mine. But don't say anything now. Think about it and we'll talk when I return from campaigning next week. By then you will have had some time to get used to the idea. Then, I promise you, I'll use every persuasive skill I've ever learned to win you over."

He gently brushed his mouth against hers again. "I don't want anything to ruin this night. Let's enjoy it without tarnishing it with doubts and common sense. It's magic, Vella. You know that as well as I do."

He had given her another reprieve, another chance to delay the inevitable. "All right," she whispered. "I'll think about it until next week."

The song the musicians were playing ended, but the notes soared on in Vella's head. Matt was right; it *was* magic, and she, of all people, knew that some things could not be changed. She had known this night would be special, but this was more than she had dared dream.

The music played on, and she allowed herself to be carried away by the mood and the moment. Matt drew her near again, and she was swept away by the warmth of his body, the glow in his eyes, and the memory of his voice telling her that he loved her.

When they had gone back to the table, he produced an elegant box from his pocket. "I have a little something for you. It's just a trinket I saw in a jewelry store, but it reminded me so much of you and the spell you've cast on me that I couldn't resist."

With trembling fingers, she took the box and opened it. Inside was the most beautiful diamond pin she had ever seen in her life.

"Oh, Matt, you shouldn't have," she murmured, a catch in her voice, tears shimmering in her eyes.

"It's nothing," he murmured, "but I wanted you to have it."

"It's beautiful," she said emotionally, "but you shouldn't have." Her fingers were trembling as she took the wand from the box and tried to pin it on her dress.

"Here, let me," he said, deftly slipping it through her dress near the left shoulder. His warm fingers brushed across her breast and Vella shivered at his intimate touch.

"It goes well with your dress," he said, his voice suddenly husky.

Vella nodded. "Beautifully," she said, glancing down at the pin, then looking up into Matt's eyes. Her hand was shaking as she traced the slim row of diamonds that formed the rod of the wand.

Drawing her hand to his lips, Matt kissed her fingers as he gazed into her eyes. "You are so very lovely that I ache for you," he said thickly.

"Oh, Matt," she murmured, wanting to tell him how much she loved him, how she longed to spend her whole life with him. But she would wait. It wouldn't be fair to do otherwise. Matt had no real idea of how their relationship might affect his future.

"Let's go," he said abruptly. "I don't want anyone else to see how badly I want you. I don't think I can hide it much longer."

Gathering up her purse, Vella hurried with him to the exit. Hand in hand, they were both laughing when they went outside and Matt summoned the valet for the car.

Unexpectedly, a man stepped out in front of them. Matt tried to shield Vella as a flashbulb went off.

"Who's the young lady, Mr. Colridge?" the photographer called out.

Matt only waved and opened the door of the car, which had been speedily delivered. The young valet was obviously used to catering to celebrities who wanted to escape in a hurry. Matt slipped him a twenty-dollar bill, opened the door for Vella, then slid behind the wheel.

"What was that all about?" Vella asked tensely, glancing back at the photographer who was running alongside the car, trying to get another shot.

Matt shrugged off the question. "I'm a public figure. Photographers seem to pop up right out of the woodwork, but that one may have been tipped off by somebody in the jewelry store. I should have been more discreet, but it doesn't really matter."

Glancing away from his glowing blue eyes, Vella chewed on her lip. A photographer, of all things!

"What will he do with the pictures?" she asked tightly.

Matt grinned. "Not a whole lot, I should think. He didn't get a decent shot."

"But what if he did?" Vella persisted.

He shrugged again. "If he's free-lancing, as many of them are, he'll try to sell a photograph to some newspaper."

When he saw the tenseness still evident in her face, he drew her against his side with one arm.

"Don't worry about it. You'll get used to this kind of thing."

Even though some inner nagging told her she *should* worry, Vella ignored it. The photographer probably hadn't gotten anything he could use, and Vella, like Matt, wanted nothing to mar this most splendid of nights. She looked down at the brilliant pin, which glittered in the scant light of the car.

"Like it?" Matt asked.

"Yes," she murmured. "Very much."

He squeezed her fingers. "I'm glad."

When they arrived back at her place, Vella invited him in. She had calmed down after the incident with the photographer, and in the comfortable silence of the car, the magic of the evening had returned.

"Can I get you a drink?" she asked, turning on a lamp as she led the way into the living room.

Matt grasped her hand before she could move too far away. His eyes were ablaze as he drew her back to him.

"You're all I want," he said in a husky voice. "All I'll ever want. I can't wait for you any longer." She intoxicated him as no drink or drug ever could. The sight of her, the scent of her, made his head reel, his pulse sing.

His mouth closed down on hers, and Vella molded herself against his hardness, completely lost in his embrace. Right now he was all that mattered to her. She had been as hungry for his touch as he had been for hers, and she wanted to savor every thrill, every provocative caress.

His lips claimed hers fiercely, longingly, making Vella suck in her breath at the intensity of his passion. His desire seemed to be suddenly un-chained; his ardor now knew no bounds.

He scattered kisses over her eyelids, her nose, her mouth. His fingers traced her lips with teasing caresses, then his mouth followed the same path, burning against hers, his tongue dipping into the sweet recesses to torment her own.

Vella was both breathless and helpless under the onslaught of his heady seduction, but she wanted nothing more than to surrender completely. His every caress, his every movement sent another shiver of delight over her skin, and she yearned to know the ecstasy of giving herself to him.

Matt's hands slid down over her back, lightly cupped her slim waist, then traced her curves beneath the full skirt of her dress. He drew her more possessively against him, his fingers pressed against her hips. He wanted to feel more and more of her; he wanted to touch her silken skin without a barrier between them, run his fingers over every part of her until he knew her intimately.

Bending his head, he let his warm lips trail down her neck to the exposed contour of her breasts. Vella leaned away from him, her eyes closed, her heart hammering beneath the burning touch of his mouth. She could feel the heat of his desire where their hips still melded and she moaned lightly in ecstasy.

Finding the zipper of her dress, Matt slid it down. The dress slipped away from her shoulders and whispered softly as it fell to the floor.

In the golden light of the lamp, Vella stood before Matt, nude except for lacy silver panties that rode down low on her slender hips. Her breasts stood firm and thrusting, the nipples dark and enticing.

"You're beautiful, so beautiful," he said, his voice deep. He exhaled raggedly as he lowered his head to taste the dark tip of one breast.

Vella cried out when his mouth closed over the rapidly tautening nipple. His tongue sent more shivers over her skin, and she locked her fingers in Matt's dark hair and tried to silence the sweet moans of pleasure that escaped her lips.

While he kissed one breast, he let his fingers circle the other, causing Vella's body to tremble with need. When she didn't think she could stand any more of his fiery seduction, Matt freed her breasts to lightly kiss the pale skin of her stomach.

"Oh, Matt, Matt," she murmured breathlessly. She was wild with wanting him, and she ached deep inside to have him become part of her and answer the call of her love.

His fingers found the elastic of her panties as he moved lower. On his knees before her, he slowly slipped the silver strip of cloth down her hips, then, parting her long shapely legs with one caressing hand, he slid the panties farther down the long length of her legs until she could step free of them.

"You're lovelier than I dreamed," he said huskily, looking up at her with fire in his eyes.

Slowly rising, he trembled as his hands continued to explore her curves. He had seen the door to her bedroom when he went up to her studio, and, abruptly, he lifted her in his arms and carried her upstairs.

When he had laid her down on the exquisite French bed, he swiftly stripped off his clothes and joined her. The blinds hadn't been closed on the upper floor, and moonlight illuminated their bodies as Matt stretched out beside her.

Silently watching him, Vella felt the wild pounding of her heart. Matt was powerfully broad and tall, potently masculine and thrilling. She reached out to him with trembling hands, and he crushed her to him hungrily, impatiently.

She pressed herself closer, relishing the feel of his hard muscles and hair-roughened body. He was the most magnificent male she had ever imagined, and her pulse quickened maddeningly as she felt his naked skin against her own. This was still like a dream to her; she could hardly believe that he was really here, making love to her.

"I want to take my time with you," he told her in a low, thick voice, "but I don't know if I can. You're the most beautiful thing I've ever seen." He laughed huskily. "Look at me. I'm trembling with desire. I've been mad for you since the first time I saw you across the room at that fund-raising dinner."

She gazed down at him, seeing his dark head against the reds, yellows, and golds of the quilt beneath him. The moonlight touched his skin with a golden caress which reflected the colors around him, surrounding him in a swirl of brightness.

Suddenly Vella felt as if she were once again seeing his face superimposed over the face of the Indian painting. All the magic was there—the colors, the intense light, the blurred edges—the blending of it all into an image so vibrant that she could never forget it.

She was trembling, too, but she couldn't find the words to tell him. She was so afraid that this was another vision, another dream that was too incredible to last. She could feel the tears build in her eyes at the wonder of the moment.

Matt's fingers were shaking as he slid them into

the dark masses of her long hair and crushed her mouth beneath his own with fervent kisses. His hands were warm and eager as they moved over her body, unable to get enough of the feel of her lovely curves.

Vella's excitement was at a feverish pitch as he stirred her passion like no other man ever had. She had been so long without love, and for so long she had imagined this man's loving. The real thing was even more tantalizing than her visions and dreams. She reached out to stroke the thick hair on his chest, and once again, she had a feeling of déjà vu as she recalled the vision she had had of herself lying naked on a bed with him, caressing his broad chest.

It required every bit of Matt's willpower not to take Vella immediately with all the force of the passion surging madly inside him, not to lower his body to hers and plunge into the depths of her loveliness repeatedly until he was finally sated.

He wanted this memory, too, to be one to treasure throughout their lifetime. With all the gentleness, the tenderness, he felt for this special woman, he rose above the frenzy of his physical desire and found a mental place that allowed him enough control to coax her desire forth until it matched his own.

When he sensed that neither of them could hang on to sanity any longer, he lowered his body to hers, and Vella gasped with pleasure as he gradually became one with her. As though their loving, too, had been written in a time long before they met, their bodies merged perfectly, breast to breast, hip to hip, thigh to thigh. With none of the awkwardness of new love, they moved together with a natural, delicious rhythm that lifted them

133

outside themselves. As the fires of their passion flared hotter and hotter, they melded together in the wonderment of a love destined by fate.

Enveloped in splendor, Vella clung tightly to Matt as he stroked her velvet warmth with his powerful masculinity, sweeping her away on waves of desire that crashed over her body, carrying her further and further from this room, this place, this time. She could feel his love flowing through her. The union with Matt was an experience as mystical as any she had ever had, and she was soon lost somewhere among the heavens as his love took her higher than she had ever thought possible.

Finally, their ecstasy exploded with more fire and brilliance than the sun and stars of the sky, filling them with showers of sensations, causing them to shudder in the throes of glorious love.

Their descent from rapture was gradual and gentle. Matt lightly rested his body on Vella's, crooning love words in her ear as he stroked her satin skin, which now glowed damply in the aftermath of their loving. For a long time, he simply enjoyed the feel of her, so warm and willing beneath him.

"I love you," he murmured at last. "I love you more than I ever thought it possible to love anyone."

"I love you, too," she whispered, relishing the sound of the words on her lips. She had wanted to tell him so many times.

Matt eased off her and rested on his side, his head supported by one hand so that he could look at Vella while he trailed the fingertips of the other down her tall, slender body.

"I wonder if I'm still dreaming," he said. "I almost can't believe you came into my life so suddenly and turned everything upside down."

"I hope you're not sorry," she whispered.

He wove his fingers into her black hair and drew her forward so that he could taste her lips again. When the sweet kiss had ended, he murmured, "How could I be sorry? You're like a gift, a treasure that fell into my world at just the right time."

Lowering her long lashes, Vella asked herself if it was indeed the right time. Or was it all wrong?

Matt slid his fingers along her spine, curving her toward his body, and she looked into his blue eyes as he dipped his head forward to claim her mouth again. She intertwined her legs with his in an automatic motion, then pressed herself against his warmth, glorying in the feel of his powerful body molding so tightly to hers.

Her fingers trailed over his muscled back, tracing his strength as they explored each hard line, then slipped down his hips to his well-defined buttocks. He was so male, so potent, and she wanted to know all of him.

When he eased her down on her back again so that he could spill kisses down her throat and breasts to her stomach, she reached out to caress his growing maleness.

"Oh, Vella," he groaned deeply, "Vella."

She could feel the throbbing start deep inside her as she stirred his passion. Her desire flared like a wind-driven brush fire, and she ached for Matt to claim her again in the mad rush of passion.

But it was not to be. This time he loved her leisurely, teasing her with his magical caresses until she thought she couldn't bear the tantalizing seduction much longer.

He crisscrossed her body with his mouth and his

fingers, all the while making her aware of his own body as he moved against her with provocative thrusts. Vella responded with a motion as old as time, rocking against him rhythmically, aching for him to ease inside her and satisfy her burning desire.

At the very moment when she was sure she couldn't keep from bursting into flames from his fire, Matt eased over on his back and pulled Vella down on top of him, her legs on each side of him.

She gasped as he filled her with his love, then she cried out his name as he cupped her derriere and controlled their loving, slowly, slowly moving her against him, sending flames shooting high inside her. Vella's fingers spread out over his chest, and she clutched at the dark hair frantically as she leaned forward, her hair spilling around both her and Matt like a cloak.

When she opened her eyes, she saw that Matt was looking at her, his lips parted, an expression of pure joy on his face. She smiled at him once as another flame of ecstasy spiraled up her body, then she closed her eyes, bit down on her lower lip and arched her back, lost almost beyond all control.

But Matt stilled her body on his, letting them both simmer down to a slow burn. Vella gazed at him through love-dimmed eyes, and she saw the gentle curve of his full mouth in the moonlight. He arched against her with the slightest of movements, while his fingers circled her nipples erotically.

Vella couldn't keep the moans from sounding in her throat, and just when she was going to plead with Matt to take her to the skies, he began all the magic again, slowly sliding her up and down on his body, until the fire burned high and still higher, and at last erupted in an explosion of rapture.

They remained joined long after the flames had burned down to smoldering embers. Matt didn't want the moment ever to end, but finally Vella moved away from him to stretch out by his side. Drawing her against him again, fitting her to the curve of his body, he wrapped his arms around her and held her as if he could not bear to let her go.

Soon they were fast asleep, joined together in love, as they both had dreamed so often. Neither of them was aware when Sneaky jumped up on the bed to join them. Ignoring both the man and the euphoric expression on the woman's face, the cat settled in beside his mistress for the night.

CHAPTER EIGHT

Vella stirred sleepily the next morning, unsure of what had awakened her. Suddenly she sat up in bed, wide-eyed. Matt! She glanced around the room, not seeing him. The faint smell of coffee lingered in the air, and she swiftly rose and pulled on her robe. Struggling to keep from stumbling over Sneaky, she made a quick trip to the bathroom to try to do something about her appearance, then hurried downstairs.

A fresh pot of coffee was still warming on the brewing stand; an empty cup sat in the sink, but there was no sign of Matt. When Vella turned toward the living room, she saw a note taped on the refrigerator door. Ripping it off, she held it in both hands to read it.

Had to run. Last night was a dream. Will call you later. Lots and lots of love.

Matt

Sighing in disappointment, Vella shut off the coffee machine. She never drank the strong brew herself, but she was glad she'd kept some on hand for guests. She had wanted to get up and prepare Matt a proper breakfast, but she had slept right through his leaving. Looking at the big copper kettle kitchen clock, she saw that it was after eight. Some romantic she was, she thought unhappily. She hadn't even realized when he took his warmth away from her.

A sweet smile curved her lips and she felt the tears building in her eyes. Last night *had been* a dream. Perhaps it was best that he had left before she awakened. In the light of day, she might have been embarrassed by the memory of her abandoned response to him.

The doorbell rang, breaking into her thoughts, and she went to answer it, Sneaky wrapping himself impatiently about her legs as he begged for his morning meal. When she pulled the door open, she saw a boy she knew from the local florist shop.

"Good morning, Miss Redding. These are for you."

He held a huge bouquet of red roses toward her, and she knew without being told that they were from Matt. The tears began to shimmer in her eyes as she took them.

"Thank you, Roy." She started to turn away. "Just a minute—"

"No need, Miss Redding," he interjected. "The sender has already provided a more than generous tip for me if I get these to you before 9:00 A.M."

She smiled at him. Matt thought of everything. "Enjoy the day, Roy."

"You, too," he said, grinning broadly as he turned away.

Vella shut the door with trembling fingers, then reached for the card on the flowers.

You're a dream. Don't vanish while I'm gone.
Love, Matt

Vella's heart was singing as she put the roses in a vase. When she had fed the cat and herself, she took the flowers upstairs with her to her studio. She found that she was in the mood to work and she didn't even bother to dress before seating herself on her stool.

Her mind full of Matt, she sat down in front of her Indian maiden and began to work as if her hands were filled with magic. Her thoughts tumbled with memories of Matt and the wonderful night they had shared, and when she thought of the magic wand pin he had given her, her mind sparkled as brilliantly as the diamonds, and she worked on, inspired as never before.

She didn't stop until almost dinnertime, and only then because Sneaky was insistent that he get some attention, and her own stomach was growling in protest. As though she were in another world, she went through the motions of a routine, then returned to her painting.

Only when fatigue demanded that she give up did she take a bath and retire. She had been in bed only a few minutes when the phone rang.

"Hello," she said expectantly.

"Vella, Matt."

"Oh, Matt," she exclaimed, unable to keep the joy from her voice. "You left before I woke up."

She could hear the warm laughter in his voice. "I know. I watched you sleep for a long time so that I could carry the memory with me. You're very beautiful. Unfortunately, I had to hit the campaign trail."

"I'm sorry you had to go," she said softly.

"So am I. I still have to finish preparing a speech tonight," he told her. "I just wanted to wish you good night."

140

"Thank you for calling," she replied, regretting that he couldn't talk longer.

"And, Vella," he murmured, "I love you. I'll talk to you soon."

"I love you, too, Matt. Good night."

She hugged the receiver to her breast for a moment before replacing it in the cradle. Then, with a smile on her lips and a dream in her heart, she closed her eyes and slipped into glorious sleep.

The morning came silently and swiftly for Vella. She was roused from her sleep by the irritating sound of the doorbell, and, barely awake, she stumbled out of bed to answer.

As she pushed her hair away from her face, she saw that it wasn't even seven o'clock. She couldn't imagine who would be calling so early. Unless it was Matt, she thought wildly, coming fully awake at once.

She flew down the stairs, Sneaky ever underfoot. When she had flung the door open, she was amazed to see Debby standing there, a paper in her hands.

"Have you seen this?" she asked breathlessly, her face flushed.

Vella stared at her blankly. "It's not even seven yet, Deb. I was still asleep."

Brushing past her friend, Debby headed to the kitchen and immediately put on a pot of hot water, the paper still tucked under her arm.

"Vella, you have told Matt, haven't you?" she asked, a frown creasing her forehead as she turned back to Vella who followed.

"What are you talking about?" Vella asked, but she knew in an instant precisely what Debby was

141

asking, and her insides shook with fear as the other woman laid the paper on the table.

"You have told him about your special talent, haven't you?" Debby asked, her voice almost pleading.

When Vella lowered her eyes, Debby sighed unhappily and flipped through the newspaper until she came to the society page. Then she silently pointed to a picture. "If you didn't tell him, I think you're in hot water now."

"Oh, God," Vella moaned, her heart almost stopping as she gazed down at the picture. The photographer had captured both her and Matt just as Matt stepped in front of her. The picture wasn't clear, but her face was fully visible over Matt's shoulder.

The caption read: "Mystery love of Matt Colridge, senatorial candidate, is local psychic."

Her legs so weak that she didn't think she could stand, Vella dropped down in the nearest chair to read the accompanying article. The color drained from her cheeks when she saw that it was an interview with her mother!

"Oh, God," she murmured. Anne Redding had not only told the reporter that her daughter, who was half Indian as well as psychic, was involved with Matt Colridge, she had also implied that she was pleased that politicians were perhaps beginning to realize the importance of the Indian cause.

"How could she?" Vella whispered tearfully. "How could she? What a way for Matt to find out the truth. Now he'll never understand why I didn't tell him myself."

Tears began to fill her eyes and spill silently down her cheeks. Debby stood behind her, just as appalled as Vella, and not knowing what to say.

The teakettle whistled shrilly, and Debby patted her friend's shoulder. "Maybe he's more understanding than you think. After all, if he cares about you, he'll realize that's not an easy thing to confess." But she couldn't hide the uncertainty in her voice. "I'll get you a cup of tea," she said quietly. What else was there to say?

Two hours later, after Matt had given a breakfast speech in a nearby town, a woman frantically waved the paper in front of him when she came up to shake his hand. Having no idea what she was talking about, he stared blankly at her as she asked him to get her an appointment with the Indian psychic.

"I'm sorry," he murmured, for once at a loss for words, "I'm afraid I don't know any Indian psychic."

Eagerly turning to the society page, the woman gestured with enthusiasm. "Yes, you do," the woman insisted, "it's right here in print. Your girl friend. Oh, please. You see, I have—"

Her voice droned on and on, but Matt did not hear. There before him was the picture of him and Vella that the photographer had snapped at the restaurant. His eyes skimmed the article, but his mind refused to believe what he was reading.

Vella, a well-known local psychic—*a fortune-teller!* Surely it was only smut, hype. She would have told him such a thing. And yet the interview otherwise seemed correct. Presumably it had been given by her own mother, Anne Redding, a woman Vella herself had said was a devout supporter of the Indian cause. And *she* had said Vella was half Indian, as well as a psychic who had helped many people with serious problems.

143

Running a weary hand through his hair, he took the paper from the woman's hands and moved away from her. "Excuse me," he murmured, leaving her to stare after him, while the other guests mulled about in confusion.

"Matt, what's wrong?"

He glanced back over his shoulder to see his campaign manager, John Ferris, coming up behind him. He shook his head, unable to explain that his whole world had just exploded in his face. Vella—a psychic. She might as well have been called a witch, and he might as well throw his hopes and dreams into the trash can with the paper.

Shutting himself in an adjoining room, he read the article very carefully, trying to understand, to digest what it could possibly mean. He loved Vella; he knew that she was unique and special, but he didn't believe in ESP and psychic phenomena.

And if she did—if she did consider herself a psychic—why hadn't she told him? She had to know that it would affect him personally, not to mention his political career. He felt somehow betrayed, as if she had made a fool of him.

His campaign manager slipped into the room, and Matt looked up, a scowl on his handsome face.

"I've made the excuse that you just heard bad news from your family," John said. "The guests have gone, but what the devil happened? You can't just walk off in the middle of an appearance with no explanation, for God's sake. What's wrong?"

Matt didn't want to talk about it, but there was no way to avoid it. Silently, he turned the newspaper so that the man could see the photo and the accompanying article.

"Oh, damn!" the shocked manager muttered without thinking. "What have you done? Surely you know that this kind of publicity can ruin you."

Matt laughed bitterly. What *had* he done? The publicity was the least of his troubles at the moment. It was the woman herself who had the power to ruin him. He had been rash, it was true. He had rushed her, but, hell, she could have been honest with him. She could have told him that there was more—much more—to her life than being a card designer.

"What kind of nut is she anyway?" John asked. "How did you get mixed up with her, of all people?"

"She's not a nut," Matt declared hotly, venting his frustration in the only way he could. He would allow no one to talk about the woman he loved that way. There had to be some explanation; before he jumped to any more conclusions, he would hear it himself.

"Cancel the rest of the day's appearances," he ordered, suddenly rising.

"You can't do that," John said frantically. "You're having lunch with the mayor."

"Cancel it!" Matt repeated, striding from the room.

"I wish there was something I could do or say," Debby murmured as she sat with a distraught Vella who was still trying to digest the article in the paper.

With tears slipping from her eyes, Vella looked at her friend. "I think I'd really like to be alone now, if you don't mind, Debby."

"No, of course not. I understand," Debby said, quickly rising. "I'll just refill your teacup." She

145

busied herself at the stove, reheating the water. When she had filled Vella's cup again, she patted her friend's shoulder once more.

Vella briefly clasped Debby's fingers to show her appreciation, then she sat drinking the tea as her friend slipped out the front door. The warm beverage did nothing at all to ease her heartache, but she waited until her tears had subsided and Debby had been gone for some time before she called her mother. She didn't know if she was more angry or hurt. She felt as if the person dearest to her had betrayed her, ruined her happiness.

Her fingers were shaking when she dialed the familiar number, and her heart sank at the sound of her mother's lively voice. She and her mother had rarely argued. Vella knew that her mother loved her, and she couldn't understand this deliberate invasion of her privacy, the thoughtless way her mother had exposed her private life.

"Mother." The word itself was an accusation.

"Arvella, what are you doing calling so early? It's not even ten, is it?"

When Vella didn't answer immediately, her mother asked, "Honey, is something wrong?"

"Have you read this morning's paper?"

"No, dear, not yet. I wasn't up when the phone rang."

"Please go outside and get it," Vella said. "I'll wait."

There was a pause on the other end of the line. "Arvella, what's this all about?" Suddenly, as if she had remembered, Anne cried, "Oh, they must have run that interview I gave. I tried to phone to tell you about it, but you weren't home."

"Yes, they ran it," Vella said tightly. "Please go and get the paper."

There was another pause, then Anne agreed. "All right. Just a minute."

Vella listened as her mother's footsteps faded. In minutes, she returned.

"What page?"

The number was etched forever in Vella's memory. "C9." She listened to the rustling of the pages as her mother located the article, and there was silence as Anne read.

Then Anne said, "All right, I've read it. It's not exactly what I said, but that's the press for you. Now why do I get the feeling that you're angry? What's wrong?"

"What's wrong?" Vella cried. "Oh, Mother, don't you know what you've done?"

Anne's voice was suddenly tinged with unease. "No, Arvella, I don't. Explain it to me."

"Why, not only have you as good as confirmed that Matt and I are involved, you've told the whole town that I'm a psychic, you've announced to the population that I'm half Indian, and you've even pleaded your Indian causes and implied that Matt feels the way you do."

For a brief time, Anne was silent, and when she eventually spoke, her voice was as full of hurt as Vella's had been. "I only told the truth, Arvella. Can you deny any of it? All right, maybe Matt Colridge doesn't care about the Indians, but he *does* care about you, doesn't he?"

"But, Mother, don't you see, don't you realize what you've done by admitting such things about my private life publicly, by using the opportunity to advocate your favorite charity?" Vella cried.

"No, Arvella, I don't. Are you ashamed of what you are? Who you are? Are you ashamed of me because I'm involved with the Indians—with your

147

people? Do you despise all the things I brought you up to believe in, all the things that make you the unique person you are?"

Her voice began to quiver with tears. "I'm sorry, Arvella. I thought I knew you better. I thought I understood you, and that you understood me. You didn't seem to me to be the kind of person to keep the truth from a man you cared about. And as for everyone else—you know as well as I do that they don't matter."

She cleared her throat and tried to continue. "I'm sorry, more sorry than you can know. If I've embarrassed you, I'm terribly sorry. I'm your mother. I love you. I never meant to hurt you. The reporter implied that he had already interviewed you and Matt and just wanted my reaction to the relationship. I didn't realize—"

Suddenly Anne began to sob softly.

"Oh, Mother," Vella murmured. "I didn't mean—"

But Anne was no longer listening. The line went dead. For a moment, Vella stood in shock, holding the receiver. What had *she* done? She was not ashamed of herself, of her heritage, of her psychic abilities, and God knew she wasn't ashamed of her mother. She had let her love for Matt and her fear of losing him color her perspective and hurt the most wonderful person in her life.

And wasn't it true that she was partly angry at her own failure to tell Matt these things herself? Would she have cared quite so much if he already knew all about her? Her mother might have been unwise to talk to the press, but she didn't deserve her daughter's fury.

How could she have been so thoughtless? Vella asked herself. She shared a very special love with her mother, and she wouldn't damage that for anything. After quickly hanging up the phone, she raced upstairs and dressed in the closest thing at hand. Then she jumped in the car and sped across town.

Her legs were trembling when she went up to her mother's front door. "Mother!" she called, not caring who heard her. "Please open the door," she pleaded as she rang the bell repeatedly.

Anne appeared immediately, tears still in her eyes.

Vella's own eyes were misty. "I'm sorry," she said. "I didn't mean to hurt you. I know that you love me and didn't mean any harm."

The two of them embraced, then Anne held her daughter away from her. "Arvella, I was foolish. I didn't realize what I was doing when I gave that interview. I'm so proud of you, honey, and I wanted everyone to know how special you are and how deserving of someone like a senator."

She looked away. "I admit I got carried away and said too much, but I didn't mean to cause you any trouble." Her eyes met her daughter's again. "You never told Matt about yourself, did you?"

Vella shook her head. "Not because I was ashamed, truly you must believe that," she said vehemently, "but because I didn't know how."

Finally, Anne had the presence of mind to close the door against the prying eyes of the neighbors. "I tried to call you back, honey. The minute I hung up, I remembered Calan and how afraid he was that someone would hear about you and think he was involved with a kook. You were afraid Matt would think the same thing, weren't you?"

Vella nodded. "I should have told him, but there

didn't seem to be any need to hurry. I've only known him for a week."

Anne shook her head. "But you knew he was the one. You told me so."

Vella agreed, and while her mother made tea, she explained her psychic visions of Matt and her belief that it would all work out somehow.

Anne was very thoughtful for a moment. Then she turned to her daughter with a smile. "It will work out, Vella. I know it. Let your mind be at rest. Your visions are never wrong. Matt and you will be together somehow eventually."

Vella, wanting to believe it, tried to return her mother's smile, but she simply didn't have Anne's confidence in this case. Fate could be fickle. And, besides, she had had her moments of love with Matt. Maybe memories were all they would ever have. She had never had a vision of a permanent relationship. That had only been a dream, which now seemed impossible.

The blood was pounding in Matt's head when he arrived at Vella's door. His emotions in turmoil, he rang the bell incessantly and called her name, but to his dismay, there was no response. He had already planned in his mind what he would say to her, and, thwarted in his attempts to get at the truth, he finally turned away.

He would try to reach Vella later in the day, but in the meantime, he would have someone check out the story. His tense posture and long strides revealing his distress, he returned to his car for the trip back across town. To his surprise, his strongest backers were at campaign headquarters when he arrived there.

And they had already done his work for him.

150

They had confirmed that Vella was not only a half-Indian psychic, but an illegitimate one to boot.

The political camp was a madhouse. His backers were both angry and upset because he had been so indiscreet about his female companion. Everyone was talking at once, trying to decide what was the best plan to offset this unfortunate incident.

"Look at this," the ex-general ground out when he saw Matt. Shaking the paper in front of the other man's face, he exclaimed, "For God's sake, we don't expect you to be celibate. We understand that you're a virile man who needs companionship, but a thing like this can ruin you—us."

"Enough!" Matt commanded, startling his illustrious supporters. "You don't even know the lady in question, and I haven't had a chance to talk with her. I must tell you that I fully intend to continue seeing her, so be very careful what you say."

Suddenly a well-known retired political leader whirled to face him. "Don't be a fool, Matt! You don't have only yourself to think of. We're trying to run a country, as you damned well know. You were selected with great care because you could contribute, and because of your impeccable war record and background. Leave this woman alone. Get away from her while you're still relatively unscathed. We'll cover this one up. Thank God the story didn't go nationwide. But we can't keep covering up if you continue to see her."

Matt could feel his blood boil. Vella had been accused and tried without a chance to defend herself. These men were insulting not only her, but him as well.

"I know what's at stake, gentlemen, just as well as you do, but I tell you this woman has been misjudged. And I also tell you that there has to be

151

more here than meets the eye. I intend to get to the bottom of it. I won't let you down," he vowed, his blue eyes blazing, "but neither will I blithely walk away from her because she might be bad for my image."

He stalked out of the room. He needed to find out what Vella had to say, but he didn't know what he would do afterward. He wasn't a fool; he knew the seriousness of what had happened.

Vella *was* a political liability, regardless of her explanation. There was no denying her background, even if the psychic story proved groundless and could easily be brushed aside. Her mother certainly wasn't an asset either. He was between a rock and a hard place. He was also hopelessly in love. The combination might very well be devastating.

CHAPTER NINE

Vella was feeling better about her mother when she returned to her house, but she was more confused than ever about Matt. She could only speculate on what he must be thinking. A thousand times, she wished that she had talked to him about herself. But, she admitted now, she had been hesitant to reveal her secret side to him. What if he had been unable to accept it? What would she have done then?

Matt himself had told her that they would talk next week when he took a break from campaigning. She had thought that would be soon enough to tell him all about her—after they'd both had time to adjust to the volatile emotions that had overcome them in the past few days. The photographer had been a fluke, just one of those things that happened, and Matt had been so sure that the man hadn't gotten a good picture.

She sat down at the kitchen table, staring vacantly at the offending newspaper article. She wondered if Matt had even seen it. Yes, she told herself; surely he had. It was the kind of thing that someone would rush to bring to his attention.

She was surprised she hadn't heard from him, but perhaps he was so angry that he wouldn't even bother to call. No, she told herself. Matt wasn't like that. He had said that he loved her, and she believed him. No matter what he thought about the story, she honestly felt that he would discuss it with her.

She was right. At four o'clock, her phone rang. Moving quickly, Vella answered it on the second ring.

"Vella, Matt. I want to talk to you. Stay right there. I'll be over in twenty minutes."

"Matt, if it's about the article—"

"It is," he interjected. "Be there."

She didn't even have a chance to say anything at all. He was very, very angry, she realized as she replaced the receiver, and she didn't know how to change that. She supposed she should try to do something about her appearance. She had left home in such a hurry this morning that she had barely bothered to run a comb through her hair.

She vacillated, wondering if he would even notice what she was wearing. He had sounded furious, and she couldn't blame him. But as she looked down at her faded jeans and T-shirt, she knew she had to change. Perhaps this would be the last time Matt would see her, and she didn't want his final memory of her to be like this. The sad thought pained her as she made her way slowly to the bathroom.

Her hair piled on top of her head, she had just stepped out of the shower when she heard the unrelenting peal of the doorbell. After hastily half drying herself, she slipped on a short robe and rushed barefoot to the door. When she opened it to greet a scowling Matt, her heart sank. He was clearly upset, and she knew it was as much her fault as her mother's.

But Matt, standing before the tall beauty, found

his anger rapidly dissipating. Despite the circumstances and his consternation, he couldn't be sensible around this woman. She was so damned appealing, standing there shoeless before him, her black hair spilling haphazardly in damp waves from the pins that had secured it. She was still wet from the shower, and her thin robe clung tantalizingly to her curves, accenting her dark nipples and slim waist.

Clutching at the short garment, Vella opened the door wide for Matt to enter. He shook his head as he stepped inside.

"Vella, Vella," he murmured, "what am I going to do about you?"

"Matt, I can explain," she said when she had closed the door behind him. She looked suddenly like a lost child, her pretty face flushed from the shower and her embarrassment.

"I hope you can, too," he said wearily, but when she held her hands out in a placating gesture, he forgot all about the trouble that had brought him here. The robe parted and he saw only this lovely creature before him, her slender figure once again luring him onto a path to magical journeys.

The madness which came over him every time he saw her stole his mind away once more. Instead of interrogating her, he wanted only to hold her in his arms and love her. He didn't know how he could question her, how he could say anything that might hurt her or insult her. She was a gift he should treasure and love. He felt that she was his destiny, no matter what her past might hold. Past and future were only words. The present was what counted.

Abruptly, he drew her against him, sliding his hands into the robe to touch her bare skin. Even as he lowered his head to taste her mouth, he told himself to be logical, to be reasonable, to take care of immediate matters. But his lips touched hers and the only really immediate matter was this woman whom he loved without conscious thought.

Lifting her in his arms, he carried her up the steps to her bedroom. Her lips clinging to his, Vella didn't utter a protest. Even if Matt walked out of her life forever tonight, she wanted to have one more memory of being in his arms. She wanted to lose herself in his precious embrace, for she was sure that she would never love again.

Neither spoke as he slipped the robe from her shoulders and cast it aside, then undressed himself. It was almost as though no further communication could occur until they had loved each other.

The real world stopped for Vella as Matt began to stroke her flesh with his hungry mouth and hands. Wanting desperately to forget that this might be the last time she saw him, she surrendered to his powerful seduction, letting her mind spin away from all thought but the whirlwind of sensations he was creating inside her. She knew only this moment, this man who could make time stop with his touch. And she relished the respite from her earlier unhappiness and confusion.

It wasn't until they lay in each other's arms in the soft afterglow of love that Matt approached the question he could not continue to ignore.

"Why weren't you honest with me?" he asked quietly, his words falling heavily in the stillness of the room.

"I was!" Vella protested, needing time to adjust to the change in his attitude. She rose up on her elbow to look at Matt, but he would not meet her eyes, so she lay back down, her posture now stiff. She was inches from him, but suddenly she felt miles away.

"Was that newspaper article true?"

She bit down on her lower lip to stop it from trembling. "Yes."

"You claim to be psychic?"

"No," she said simply. "I don't claim to be. I am."

Matt seemed to digest the statement for a moment. "Just what is it that you do, Vella?"

Vella pondered the question, not really knowing how she should answer. Struggling with the words she wanted to say, she murmured, "All my life I've seen things that other people haven't. My mother knew it by the time I was five years old, and she encouraged me to develop what she feels is a God-given talent, inherited from my father, who also had visions."

She lowered her long lashes. "Those things aren't rare with the Indians, as you must know. They would be less rare with the rest of us if we would open ourselves up to them."

Shifting uneasily beside her, Matt exhaled wearily. "What do you see?"

"I see the future for some people. For example, the woman who sat across from you at dinner at Debby's. She asked me to meditate about her daughter's job change because it was causing family dissention. Some of the problems are as simple as that. Sometimes they are much more complicated and far-reaching."

Matt suddenly remembered part of the conversation he had overheard between Vella and the woman, LaVerne Morris, and he recalled thinking that Vella had helped her in some way.

Vella told him about her visions, her advice, and the outcome. Drawing in a tired breath, Matt forced himself to listen to the woman he loved while she spoke on an idea that went against all the things he had ever believed in. All his life he had shunned such things as extrasensory perception. He had always thought psychics to be little more than charlatans, exploiting people's credibility and their desire to believe in something more. At the very most, he had considered psychic experiences to be coincidences.

Yet, as he lay by Vella's side, he knew that she believed in her own powers. Hadn't he also believed she was special, different, from the very first moment he saw her? But it was difficult, if not impossible, for him to understand that she sincerely believed she could see anyone's future.

"Why didn't you tell me this before?" he asked tightly. "You must have known that this side of your life would affect my career."

"I wanted to tell you so many times," she said hesitantly. "I tried to bring up the subject, even on our first date."

Her gray eyes were shining with unhappiness when she looked at him. "But I felt you wouldn't believe me. You were so adamant in your belief about life consisting of the here and now that I couldn't risk hearing you dismiss as impossible something that is so precious to me."

Abruptly, he remembered the conversation they had had the first night he took her to dinner. She had said something about worlds beyond what we see and touch, but he hadn't really placed any significance on it. Clearly that had been a mistake, a mistake he would pay dearly for, because, as he listened to her, he became increasingly miserable.

158

He had been right to be wary of her when she forthrightly told him her attitude about politicians. Her dislike of politics had been bad enough, but her background could be even more threatening: an illegitimate half-Indian psychic. She was a politician's nightmare. And he was in love with her!

He should have trusted his instincts and left her alone. He glanced at Vella and saw that she was staring at him with those fathomless gray eyes, and he remembered why it had been impossible to do the wise thing where she was concerned.

And now—now he was in way over his head. In fact, he had completely lost his heart to this unusual woman. What could he do about this difficult situation? He and Vella were as different as day and night. Could even a love as fierce as his overcome their differences?

He could not forget how futilely he had struggled to make a go of his first marriage. Was he destined to repeat that painful mistake? Or would he be strong enough to walk away from this woman now and save them both untold heartache?

He felt inadequate, incapable of making such a potentially devastating decision. "Let's go get something to eat," he said unexpectedly. He had to think, to be occupied in areas outside Vella's magical sphere.

He and Vella dressed in silence. And, still silent, lost in their own aching world, they went out the front door.

Suddenly two reporters and a photographer appeared out of nowhere. "Hey, give us the scoop, Mr. Colridge," one called out as Matt tried to whisk Vella down the sidewalk to his car. "Is this the real thing? Is the next California senator going to marry the fortune-teller?"

"Hell," Matt muttered sourly beneath his breath. Putting a smile on his face, he glanced back at the reporter who was close on his heels. "No comment yet," he said with incredible charm. "When there's a story, we won't keep it a secret." But his fingers were biting painfully into Vella's arm as he helped her into the car.

"It's too late for that now," the man said, following Matt around the car. "Come on, give us a break. Will there be a wedding?"

Cringing at the reporter's persistence, Vella wished she could vanish. *Fortune-teller*, he had called her. Not that she hadn't heard the term applied to her before, but suddenly, in connection with Matt, it sounded more tawdry than usual.

And in a flash, she fully realized how much she could damage Matt's chances to become the California senator. She had thought of that before, too, but now the reality struck her like a forceful blow in the chest. Why had she let things get out of hand? Why had she let this happen? Hadn't she learned anything at all from Calan and his fears?

Matt stomped on the gas pedal and sped away before the reporters could get in their car and follow, but the evening was already ruined, the glow gone from the love they had shared earlier.

When they had been seated in a secluded corner of a tiny little nondescript restaurant and had ordered hamburgers and Cokes, Matt ran his hands through his hair tiredly.

Vella looked away from him, knowing that she had to say the words that would break her heart. There was no point in prolonging the agony for either of them.

160

"I'm sorry, Matt," she said. "The situation is impossible. *We're* impossible. You're in one world and I'm in another, and there really is no way for them ever to meet."

Matt reached out to take her hand in his, causing her to look at him. Then he shook his head unhappily. "They've already met, Vella. It's too late for rationalizing. I'm in love with you."

"But it won't work!" she cried passionately. "You must see that now." Suddenly she couldn't bear it any longer. She rushed from the room, tears falling from her eyes.

Matt threw some money down on the table and ran after her. When he caught her outside on the darkened street, he drew her firmly against him, letting her sob against his shirt.

But there was no way he could console her. It was too late for that. When her tears had subsided, she looked up at him beseechingly.

"Please take me home, Matt."

Hugging her to his side, he guided her back to the car. Once inside, Vella sat rigidly on the passenger side, not speaking as they rode back to her house. When Matt had parked the car, she looked away from him.

"I don't want to see you again, Matt," she forced herself to say. "We both know it's best."

Before he could stop her, she got out and ran into her house. Her tears almost blinding her, she stood by the front window, watching as Matt sat in the car for a few minutes. He looked like a man defeated, broken. Finally he started the engine and drove off.

Vella stared after him until the car vanished. When it was completely gone from sight, she collapsed on the couch where Matt had first made love to her. Curling up into an aching ball of misery, she sobbed as if her heart were literally breaking.

Her mother had been wrong. It wasn't better to have known those few ecstatic hours in the arms of the man she loved. They would only remind her of what she might have had, if she weren't a psychic . . . if he weren't a politician. The tears fell faster and harder, and Vella sobbed until she was gasping for breath.

How could it be? Why had she dreamed of him for so long? What good were those moments of insight if they brought only unhappiness to her? Was it her destiny to help solve other people's problems but never her own? Why did she have the power to see another woman's future while she could only stumble blindly toward her own fate?

Or, was she, like her mother, to sample a brief and exquisite ecstasy and live forever on the memory? Anne had done it, but Vella didn't see how she could survive that way. And what was she to do with all the love she felt for the man who had so briefly made real her waking dream? She curled her body more tightly, seeking refuge, comfort. But there was none to be found. She hurt so much that she didn't think she could bear it. What was the point in going on without Matt?

She was startled from her woe by the fierce pounding on her door. Gasping, she brushed at her tears and struggled to straighten up. As she listened, she was sure she heard Matt calling out to her.

"Vella. Vella."

Was it only in her mind, or had he come back? He called her name again, and when she realized

162

that he was at her door in the flesh, her heart sang. But it was only for an instant.

For a long time she let the tortured sound of her name on his lips wash over her. Why hadn't he gone away, as she had asked him to? Why was he making this harder when it already was impossible? He knew it couldn't work. She knew it too. They had had their moment in time. He belonged to the public, and she belonged in her secret world that few other people could ever understand.

"Vella, please."

Her heart ached at his ragged plea. Against all her better instincts, she stumbled to her feet and raced to open the door for him.

"Vella, Vella," he murmured hauntingly, pulling her into his arms. "Don't do that again. Don't ever walk away from me like that. We'll make this work somehow. We'll try to understand each other's different philosophies. I swear my love for you is so deep that it will overcome anything."

He spun her wildly around the room as though he had come home after a long and bitter war. "When I thought about never seeing you again, I wanted to die."

Through her laughter and tears, Vella confessed that she had felt the same way, but inside she cautioned her heart. After all, she knew nothing had changed.

"You can't have both politics and me, Matt," she said solemnly when he had put her back on her feet. She could see how the thought pained him.

"I can if you love me enough to compromise a little," he heard himself saying.

He bit down on his tongue. Why was he asking this? Hadn't he vowed that never again would he try to change anyone? But, he soothed his conscience, he wasn't trying to change her. He was only asking that she work with him on this thing, see it through with him.

"What kind of compromise?" she asked earnestly, willing to do almost anything to keep him —in spite of the odds.

He wiped at the traces of her tears. "Vella, if you'll only stay out of the limelight, I will appease my disgruntled backers. Let me get through the campaign without further incident. When everyone gets to know you, they'll realize what a wonderful woman you are, but there's no denying that articles like that one in the paper will damage my candidacy."

"My mother didn't realize all the harm she could do," Vella said softly, walking with Matt to the couch. "She's so dedicated to the Indians—to my people," she amended, "that she got carried away when the reporter approached her. She won't do that again."

"Oh, Vella," he groaned unhappily, "I don't want to be in the position of trying to restrict your, or your mother's, freedom. Please understand that. But I honestly think I have something to offer the country. I believe I can do something to help people. I think I understand the average man as most other politicians don't. I've geared my entire life in that direction."

Vella shushed him with her finger. "Don't apologize. I understand the difficulty of the situation." She lowered her dark lashes. "Please believe that I am not some crazy publicity seeker."

Her mysterious gray eyes met his. She winced when she thought of the conversation between her mother and herself on the phone, and how she had very nearly tried to deny who and what she

was. She never wanted even to come close to doing that again. She had long accepted her special
talent, despite the world's view of psychics, but
she could empathize with Matt's struggle.

"I won't deny my help to anyone who seriously
needs it, Matt, but I don't go out of my way to
advertise my talents. I want you to understand
that."

He did want to understand it. He wanted to
understand her and the secrets in her wide gray
eyes. He realized, as she did, that they needed
more time, time to adjust to this new dimension of
their lives, to accept each other's different philosophies.

Vella still found Matt naive in his political thinking. She realized that he truly believed that he, a
lone man, could have some effect on the country,
make some impact on the long-established political customs, and benefit the average citizen. Calan
had believed it at a very early age, and Calan had
been wrong. But she wanted desperately to believe what Matt believed. She loved him so passionately, so blindly, that she was willing to try to
compromise in order to make their relationship
work.

There seemed to be nothing more to say at the
moment. Matt's dark blue eyes searched Vella's
tear-streaked face, and his heart hurt for her. He
didn't want to be the cause of any unhappiness,
any embarrassment, for her.

He recalled how extraordinary he had thought
her to be the night he met her. Despite the recent
revelations—or maybe even because of them, he
conceded—he still found her extraordinary, a
woman with inner beauty and dignity, as well as a
passionate, giving nature that was incredibly rare.

He leaned over to kiss away the hints of moisture that remained on her face, and his lips soon found her mouth. Vella was the one to pull away first, and this time *she* took his hand and led him to her bedroom.

She yearned to lose herself in his lovemaking, to forget how she had thought she had lost him forever and had no reason to go on. She wanted him to stroke away her misery, to set her heart and body free as only he could do. If only one more time—

CHAPTER TEN

Vella awakened to the feel of Matt's lips on hers.

"Good morning, sleepyhead," he said in a low voice when she opened her eyes wide in surprise.

"Oh, Matt," she murmured. "Good morning. I thought I was dreaming."

"I've thought I was dreaming ever since I met you," he whispered. "But I know now that no dream could ever be this wonderful."

When she smiled at him, Matt kissed her again, then slipped from beneath the sheet. "I've got to run. I have appointments, and after skipping out yesterday, I better not do it again."

Vella watched with pleasure in her sleepy eyes as Matt walked toward the bathroom, his broad hairy shoulders, narrow waist, and muscular legs making her long to feel his body against hers again. Shaking the thought from her head, she quickly got up and pulled a robe on.

"The towels on the rack are clean," she said through the closed door of the bathroom. "If you want to shower, please do. And you can use one of the disposable razors in the top drawer of the cupboard."

Matt opened the door and grinned at her before she could move away. "You make a mighty fine hostess," he said. "Do you have a toothbrush I could use? Then I won't have to go by my place at all. I'll wear what I wore yesterday." He winked. "That's the beauty of meeting a whole new group of people."

"There's a new red toothbrush in the top drawer. I haven't used it."

"Great. I'll be out in a few minutes."

When he had closed the door, Vella hurried downstairs and quickly started a breakfast of poached eggs on English muffins and fresh fruit. She had everything ready, including a steaming cup of coffee for Matt, when he came down.

Coming up behind her as she turned toward the table, two glasses of milk in her hands, Matt wrapped his arms around her and kissed the back of her neck.

"No fair," she said with a giggle. "I've got my hands full."

"So have I," he said. "And I love it."

When he had freed her, he joined her at the table and ate his breakfast in haste.

"Got to run," he said. "Thank you for the meal. It was very good. I think I'm going to like being a vegetarian."

Then he leaned over to lift a quick kiss from her lips and he was gone. Vella looked after him, smiling easily. It was almost possible to believe that yesterday and the article hadn't happened at all. After she cleaned off the table and fed Sneaky, she went upstairs to dress, then went immediately to her workroom.

She was lost in her creation and thoughts of Matt when the phone rang. Absently picking it up, she said hello.

"Vella, this is Captain Nash down at the precinct. Listen, honey, we've got a situation here. A four-year-old girl has been missing overnight without a trace. I know I don't usually call you in on something like this so soon, but the parents of the child are friends of mine. It may be a simple case of the girl wandering off, but we've had searchers out to no avail. Will you do me this favor and come down and see if you can help us out?"

"Yes, of course," Vella said without hesitation. She had helped locate missing persons on other occasions. It was a request she would not deny under any circumstances. "I'll be there as quickly as I can."

"Thanks, honey. You're a doll."

The image of Matt's face crossed Vella's mind only fleetingly as she made her way down to the police station. When she arrived, the captain took her into a secluded room and showed her pictures of the child and explained what had led up to her disappearance. Then he left Vella alone so she could meditate.

When he came back to check on her later, she was still drawing a blank. "I'm sorry. I can't see a thing," she said tiredly. The intense concentration was very draining, and she felt quite weak.

Captain Nash was familiar with how she worked. "How about a cup of hot tea with some sugar?"

She nodded. "That would be nice."

"Better yet," he said, his craggy face breaking into a smile, "why don't I treat you to lunch? Have you eaten?"

She shook her head. "I don't even know what time it is."

"After twelve. Listen, why don't I make arrangements with the mother for you to see the child's room?"

Vella nodded. "I think it might help."

After she and the captain had eaten lunch in a little diner down the street from the station, he drove her to one of the nicer parts of town.

"You don't feel this is a kidnapping for ransom?" Vella asked.

Captain Nash shook his head. "Our first thought was kidnapping, but there have been no calls. Not that it has been ruled out completely this soon, of course. We don't know what to think yet. The parents are frantic, I don't need to tell you."

Vella could just imagine how agonized the family of the child was. "I'll do all I can," she said unnecessarily.

When she and the captain were admitted, the mother of the child rushed up to them, her face white, her eyes puffy from crying. "Are you the psychic?" she asked wildly.

"Yes, Anita," the captain said. "This is Vella Redding."

"Oh, can you help find my baby?" the woman begged. "It was my fault, you see. There was a birthday party in the park for one of the neighborhood children. Peggy was playing with them on the swings. I was talking with the other mothers." She shook her head. "It happened so fast. One minute she was there, and the next she wasn't. I should have kept watch." She began to sob hysterically, and a man appeared to take her in his arms.

He, too, was pale and red-eyed.

"Vella Redding, this is Neels Ashton."

"Just go on into Peggy's room," the man said over the sobbing woman's head.

Vella felt an intense rush of pain for this stricken family, and she silently prayed that she could do something to help.

170

The nursery was on the second floor, and when she stepped inside, she instantly felt the presence of the child. She smiled unconsciously to herself. That usually meant that the person was still alive. The captain waited outside while Vella walked around the room, getting a feel for the little girl who had spent so much of her life there.

Automatically, she examined the little dresses in the closet and stroked the pretty sweaters. Then she ran her hands over the bed where the child had slept. Finally, she examined the child's toys.

"This one was—is—her favorite," the father said, coming into the room beside Vella.

For a moment she was startled out of her meditation. She began to lose the vibrations, and, as if sensing that he had intruded inopportunely, the man handed her a worn teddy bear and left.

Standing in the middle of the room, Vella pressed the bear to her breast and closed her eyes. For a long, long time, she saw nothing at all, but she knew that she was on to something just the same. Just as when she was lost in her painting, a certain feeling came over her, and she struggled to make it work for her.

She had no idea how long she stood in the room, quiet and still, the rest of the world nonexistent for her, but gradually, slowly, she began to get distorted pictures in her mind. They had something to do with metal or aluminum and motion.

Was it cars? she wondered. She shook her head, unable to grasp the foggy symbol. There was cement in the background. Was it a road? Or perhaps a factory?

Again she unconsciously shook her head, knowing that she was on the right track, but unable to comprehend the significance of the hazy image.

Eventually it became a little clearer. She could see a sign in front of a vague structure. She strained to read the words, but they were blurred and elusive, dancing teasingly before her eyes.

She sucked in her breath. Once, when the sign moved, she saw the face of a child. A shiver raced over her skin. Peggy Ashton. She was sure of it. She concentrated more intensely. Her hands began to perspire on the dark fur of the teddy bear she clutched to her bosom.

Again she sensed that metal and motion were involved. She tried to stay with that thought now. Moving metal. Cars? Trailers? A building with a sign. A trailer court?

She tried again to stay with the image of the building. The sign moved eerily before her eyes, again giving her a glimpse of a child. This time she saw that the girl was young and blond. She seemed to be sleeping. Her eyes were closed and her face dirty and tear-streaked. Again she told herself that it was Peggy Ashton. But where was she?

Vella's clothes grew damp on her body and her legs began to tremble, but she couldn't leave the vision. The sign moved and the letters flashed before her eyes. Mobile. Was it a gas station? Could that be the reason for the cars and motion? No, that wasn't it. She was sure it wasn't.

She continued to stroke the toy bear's fur. As though it was an extension of her fingers, another image grew in her mind. Fur. A cat. The child and a cat. But what did it mean?

She concentrated until her head felt overfull with images. A metal building. Cement. There was more cement in her sight now. Patches of it. No—slabs. A sign with the word Mobile.

She was getting closer. She could feel it. Her

thoughts began to tumble over each other as a more complete image formed. A mobile home park! That was it!

But suddenly it was gone. All of it. The vision vanished as irrevocably as if it had never been. Exhausted, Vella bowed her head and tried desperately to recapture it. But she knew it was no use.

Very slowly, she opened her eyes. Captain Nash appeared at her side to help her to the child's bed.

"Lie down," he said gently, knowing the trauma she had gone through to try to locate the child. He helped her sip a glass of cool water.

Vella closed her eyes again. She was so weak she didn't think she could ever move again. Her head was spinning now, and she felt sick and dizzy.

For some time she lay on the bed, trying to step from one world back into the other. At last she opened her eyes again, and she felt more normal. She could focus.

"Did you get anything?" he asked anxiously.

She nodded, aware that she should not discuss it in front of the family.

"Good."

He helped Vella up from the bed. "Are you okay?" he asked.

When she had assured him that she was, he led her from the room, past the anguished parents, and out to the street. On the way back to the station, Vella told him what she had seen.

"And you think the child's alive?" he asked eagerly.

"Yes, I do."

He squeezed her hand. "Thanks, doll. I don't need to tell you how much we all appreciate your help. I'm going to put some men on this right away. I just hope we get a location in time."

"So do I," Vella whispered prayerfully. "So do I."

"Want me to drive you home?" he asked as they parked in front of the station.

She shook her head. "No, thanks. I can manage."

"How about dinner before you go?"

She shook her head again. "I'm not hungry, thank you."

"You sure you're going to be all right?"

She nodded again. But she wasn't all that sure, and instead of going home, she went to her mother's house, where, for two days she slept almost constantly, only waking at her mother's insistence to drink liquids and eat soup.

On the third day Anne woke her to tell her the child had been found in a new mobile home park just being set up. Only a few spaces were already occupied, and Peggy Ashton had apparently followed a kitten from the park to one of the existing homes on the back of the lot. She had squeezed in through an opening in the coach skirting. Then she had slid the skirting closed and had been unable to open it again from the inside.

The police had searched that area, but the coach was so far away from the other occupied ones that no one in the 300-space park had heard her cries. Apparently, in her panic in the darkness, she had collided with one of the heavy trailer supports and been knocked unconscious.

"Is she all right?" Vella asked anxiously.

"Yes, she came around just yesterday. She was terrified, of course, but she's going to be all right. Who knows what would have happened if she hadn't been found? You did a great thing, Arvella. You saved that little girl's life."

"Thanks, Mother," Vella said softly, but both of them knew she didn't need any praise. Finding the child was reward enough.

Anne Redding lowered her eyes, and Vella stared at her questioningly. "What aren't you telling me?"

Anne couldn't meet her daughter's gaze. She took Vella's hand in hers and lightly caressed it. "You've made the papers again," she said tensely. "This time a weekly tabloid."

"Oh, God," Vella wailed. "How? Why? Oh, surely not over the child!"

Pained blue eyes met angry gray ones. "Yes, I'm afraid so. It's pretty bad, dear. You've gotten national headlines."

"Oh, please, no," Vella whispered, tears coming to her eyes. Who had done this? "I know Captain Nash would never let it leak. He and I have an agreement." She could feel her stomach muscles tighten as a picture of Matt flashed into her mind. She had been *sure* no one would hear about this incident, and yet she had made the papers again.

Anne shook her head. "I don't know who, Arvella, but I warn you that the piece is unflattering."

Vella sat up against the headboard of the bed. "Let me see it, Mother."

Anne knew there was no point in ignoring the request. She watched as her daughter cringed at the headline, repeating it aloud as though she honestly couldn't believe it.

"Senate Hopeful Matt Colridge Tied to Illegitimate Indian Psychic Who Found Missing Child."

The accompanying article was filled with gossipy bits of speculation about Matt's involvement with her, even hinting that the missing child was a publicity stunt drummed up by Matt's campaign manager to give credence to Vella's psychic abilities. Vella blanched at lines which suggested that she might read the future for California Senator Matthew Colridge with smoke signals and crystal balls.

"Matt tracked you here," Anne said with reluctance. "He's been calling incessantly, Arvella. He wants to see you. The only reason he hasn't come is because I've told him I won't let him in."

Vella looked up at her mother with pained eyes. "Will you get Captain Nash on the phone, please?"

"He's already called. He said he was deeply sorry about this. One of his men inadvertently let it leak to a friend who worked for Matt's opposition. He said to assure you that the man has been chastised."

"Chastised," Vella repeated unhappily. "He's been chastised while the country laughs at Matt."

"Matt will understand that you don't have any control over this kind of thing," Anne insisted. "Surely he won't hold you accountable."

Vella looked at her mother, tears shimmering in her eyes. "It doesn't matter, Mother. Don't you see that Matt and I have no chance." She looked away. "We never did, really. I'm a political handicap. I could eventually ruin all his chances to become a senator—if I haven't already."

"Call him, Arvella. He left his number. You need to talk to him."

With a weary sigh, she nodded. "All right."

Vella had the feeling that Matt was waiting by the phone for her call. He answered immediately.

"Hello."

"Matt—"

The sound of his name on her lips caused Matt to draw in his breath. What bewitching power did she have over him? He loved her, without a doubt, but she was poison. His backers had been livid when the second piece followed so swiftly and scandalously after the first.

They had demanded that he disengage himself from this albatross while there was still some hope of redeeming himself with the public. They strongly suggested that he immediately ally himself with a woman of political influence and good reputation and propose marriage, if only to get himself through the campaign period.

Vella could hear him sigh heavily when he recognized her voice, but he only said, "Hello, Vella."

She hardly knew what to say herself.

"Matt, I suppose you've seen that tabloid."

"Hasn't the whole country?" he asked tartly. "I suppose you have a logical explanation."

Vella bristled at the accusation in his tone. "Yes, if you truly feel that I owe you one under the circumstances."

He did, and he wanted to hear it. His mind demanded that he hear it over the phone, away from Vella's intoxicating presence, but he found himself saying, "I do. May I come over to your mother's house? I don't think either your place or mine is safe now."

Safe, Vella thought. Safe from what? Snooping neighbors and prying reporters? They weren't the danger. The danger was the attraction between her and Matt, and their respective interests. The combination was explosive and destructive. It was impossible.

"I'm sorry for the disruption of your life, Matt,"

she said wearily. "Why don't we just call it a day. You don't need an explanation from me."

Matt knew that she was right; he didn't need one, but he wanted one. She was also right that they should simply call it a day. He was throwing over his entire future for this woman. But what would his future be without her?

He ran his hands through his hair. He didn't know what to think, what to believe anymore. He had always mapped his life out so carefully. Maybe his supporters were right; maybe he would get over Vella eventually. Perhaps he should listen to them. Perhaps. But he had to see Vella once more. He couldn't let it end like this.

"I have your mother's address. What time shall I come?"

Vella clutched the phone with both hands. Why was he insisting? And why was she going to give in?

"In half an hour."

"All right." There were no mentions of love now. Matt hung up without another word, and Vella quietly returned the phone to its cradle.

Anne was watching her daughter anxiously. "What did he say?"

"He's coming over. Do you have something I can put on?" She had slept in her clothes the first day, and they weren't fit to wear.

"Of course," Anne replied. She returned minutes later with one of her nicer outfits accented by an Indian belt.

The irony made Vella want to both laugh and cry. With a bittersweet smile on her lips, she went to the bathroom to take a shower.

When Matt arrived, she was dressed in a red cotton blouse, a black skirt with a ribbon of red

178

around the hem, and a black belt decorated with silver coins. She had done her hair in two braids.

"Come in," she said quietly, all her bitterness melting at the sight of his haggard face.

Matt felt his insides tighten when he saw her. She held his heart and future in her hands, and he didn't know what he would do about it. He only knew that he loved her beyond all reason.

CHAPTER ELEVEN

Vella turned toward her mother. "Mother, this is Matt Colridge. Matt, my mother, Anne Redding."

Matt automatically held out his hand, intrigued by the woman who had produced such an unusual daughter. He was surprised to see that she was dressed so quaintly. He didn't know why anything surprised him now, and he had to admit that the sight was somehow very pleasing. She had a serene face that echoed some of Vella's features, but clearly the daughter had gotten most of her looks from her Indian father.

"I'm glad to finally meet you," Matt said, and he suddenly remembered how eager he had once been to know this woman. But that seemed like a long, long time ago now. His world had spun on its axle several times since, turning him upside down.

"Likewise," Anne said politely, then she vanished down the hall on silent feet.

Matt stared after her as she disappeared. Then he looked back at Vella. It was all he could do not to take her in his arms, but he would not allow himself to fall prey to such thoughts.

"Won't you sit down?" she asked, indicating a small orange couch.

"Thank you." The length of the couch necessitated that they sit close, but they were as stone statues locked in remote poses.

Vella licked her lips, wanting to get this painful confrontation over with. She had been wrong to prolong the affair after the first article.

"What happened this time? Are you going to tell me how you wound up in the papers again after you promised to stay out of the limelight?" Matt asked harshly before Vella could speak. He could feel the anger surge in his body, and he knew that he was directing his weakness for this woman into hostility.

Vella turned on him, her eyes blazing. She was just as much a victim of this as he was, and she would not suffer his arrogant attack.

"Until I met you, Matt Colridge, the papers never bothered to notice me. *Never.* I don't like this any more than you do."

For a moment he was taken aback by her attitude, but only for a moment. "Then why did you do it?"

"Do what?" she demanded tightly, her own anger singing in her veins. "Save a child's life? What would you have done if you had the power to help?" Her fury was fueled by her own helplessness. She loved Matt, and all this pain and misery shouldn't be happening.

"You talk about wanting to help the oppressed, the needy," she cried. "Well, there is more to helping than just dealing with the physical needs of people. What about mental anguish? I have a God-given talent to see what most other people can't. A child was missing, for heaven's sake! Can you even begin to imagine her parents' agony? I'm proud that I could do something to relieve it. I'm grateful that I could help. What did you expect me to do?"

Matt gazed at her incredulously for a moment. He would not insult her by asking her if she had really found the child. He believed that she had. He didn't understand it, but he believed it. And, yes, of course, if he had the power, he would have done the same thing.

"But why did you let the papers know?" he persisted. "They've turned you into a freak. They've made a three-ring circus out of our relationship."

"I didn't do it," she declared vehemently, appalled that he could even think such a thing. "Your opposition did it. I told you I've never been in the papers before. I've worked with the police for years, and never, until you were involved in my life, have I been made to look like a freak."

Matt shook his head, unable to absorb all that she was saying. Abruptly he drew her into his arms. God, had he done this to her by involving himself in her life? He recalled how he had once thought she seemed at ease with life, as though she knew the secrets of the universe. What was he doing to this unique, incredible woman he admired so much? She was as distraught as he, and equally innocent of any wrongdoing.

Of course she had a right to be proud of her talent. He was proud of her, too, but he, of all people, knew that the American public wasn't ready for a politician who was involved with a psychic. He didn't know which way to turn: he wanted both Vella and his career, but they made poor bedfellows.

Vella moved closer to him, needing his strength now, needing his understanding, and knowing in her heart that she was trying to hold on to an impossible dream. She was what she was, and he was what he was. The incident with the child had opened her eyes even wider.

She was only doing what Matt claimed to want to do, helping people in need, but his was an acceptable kind of help. Hers was not. She knew now that she was selfish to cling to him, to try to keep him for herself. She truly believed that he had something real and rare to contribute to politics.

And she had something to contribute to the world, in her own way. She would not deny her psychic abilities to save herself from the doubters and scoffers and hecklers. She had saved a child's life, and she would not be ashamed of it, despite the laughter and ridicule now directed at her. She would not turn her back on what she was. Not even for Matt.

Though it hurt her as nothing ever had before, she knew that she had to let him go. She had finally realized that they both had more to offer the world singly than together. Pulling free of his arms, she looked into his tormented blue eyes.

"This is all wrong, Matt," she said as evenly as possible. "It's been wrong from the first. I never should have become involved with a politician."

"Vella," he began, "somehow we have got to make this thing work. I love you too much to let you go."

She shook her head and lowered her eyes so that he couldn't see the forming tears. "I don't want you, Matt. I realize that now." When her eyes met his, they were remarkably dry. "I don't want to be involved with your kind of man. I was engaged once to an aspiring politician. I tried desperately to understand and accept his career, but I could not. Neither can I accept yours now." At least that much wasn't a lie, she told herself.

183

She didn't add that Calan had been more ashamed of her psychic abilities than Matt appeared to be. Nor did she add that Calan had been broken by his idealism.

"I don't want to see you again. I mean it. Please don't try to contact me again. We've already done enough damage to each other."

"You don't mean that, Vella," he insisted, trying to draw her back into his arms. "I'm the first to admit that the whole thing is a mess now, but it'll work itself out. I'll give up politics if that's what you want—if it means not losing you."

It was the last thing she wanted. She wasn't a fool. She would never ask that of him. He wouldn't be the man he was without his dreams and his plans. She had to find a way to turn him from her.

"You don't understand, Matt," she said, unable to meet his eyes. "I don't want your kind of life. I could never live in a goldfish bowl with people prying and poking at me. I won't change, and you shouldn't either. Neither of us will ever be happy as less than what we are."

"Don't sit there and speak so rationally and coolly to me after you've driven me wild," he said with sudden fire. Vella saw the steel, the determination, beneath the charm of the politician, the warmth of the lover, the wrath of the man. "Don't tell me you can walk away from me again without looking back. I won't believe it. I won't hear it."

He drew her forward to kiss her mouth passionately. Vella fought to hang on to whatever strength she had left, but it was with great difficulty that she resisted his caresses. She loved him so deeply.

At the moment she was sure she loved him enough never to look into anyone else's future but her own, and yet she knew there was no turning

184

back. She would not ask Matt to change himself for her.

Finally she struggled free of his arms. "Don't, Matt. That won't help."

Stricken, he stared at her. "Can you sit there and tell me that you don't love me, Vella?"

Biting her lip until she was sure she could taste blood, she struggled to tell him the lie. "I don't." There was no way she could say all the words.

"You do," he insisted, grabbing her by her shoulders as if he could shake some sense into her.

"No," she whispered huskily. "I've known nothing but heartache since I met you. Let me go back to my private life. I don't want to be part of yours."

Suddenly he pushed her away as though she had slapped him. How dare she turn him around and around, then turn him loose to spend his days without her? How dare she bewitch him, then spurn him? His life had been just as upset as hers, but he loved her above all else. It had been worth the pain, the consternation, the confusion—at least to him.

"Please, Matt," she whispered. "Just go away."

He staggered to his feet, shattered because she didn't want him at any cost. Nothing he said or did had changed her mind, and she had finally damaged his pride, his dignity. As though he couldn't believe what he had heard, he turned away from her without speaking. His legs leaden, he somehow made his way to the door and out on the street.

For a long time he sat in his car in front of the apartment building trying to digest what she had said. He could accept anything but the fact that she didn't love him.

Finally, numb with grief, he drove back to his

condominium. For hours he sat on his couch, trying to accept what Vella had said. But he couldn't. He *wouldn't.* He didn't believe that she didn't love him. He had felt it, known it. She was trying to give him back to his career without the complications she had brought to his campaign.

Damn her! he thought furiously. She couldn't so easily rid herself of him. He wanted her forever. And he was not a man to give up so readily. What was he running away from? Vella? God knows he wanted her, and, recovering from the blow to his pride, he told himself that he truly believed she wanted him.

He had to talk to her, to make her see what she was throwing away. When he called her mother's house, he was told that Vella had gone. But when he tried to reach her at home, he got no answer. He tried intermittently for the next hour, then drove over. He received no answer at the door either. But, he vowed, she couldn't hide from him forever. He would give her the night to calm down, then he would talk to her tomorrow.

Her heart aching, Vella rushed home immediately after Matt drove away from her mother's house. But she didn't want to stay where he had made such beautiful love to her. She needed to find someplace where she wouldn't see him, think of him, dream of him everywhere she turned.

She had often spent time at Debby and Sam's mountain retreat, and, after she had sworn Debby to secrecy, she asked if she could spend some time there. Concisely, she explained the situation with Matt.

"If I don't get away, Deb, I'll go crazy," she confessed.

186

"You know you can stay anytime," Debby said sympathetically. "But are you going to be all right?"

"Yes, I'll have to be, won't I?" Vella asked tearfully.

"Oh, Vella, it's too late to tell you I told you so, isn't it?" her friend asked.

Vella tried to laugh, but she hurt too much. "You can say it, but it won't do any good."

"You really love him, don't you?"

It had been hard enough to deny it to Matt; there was no point in lying to her friend. "More than anything in life, Debby, but we've caused each other enough pain. There is no way we can have a life together."

"I'm sorry, Vella," Debby said. She was clearly struggling to say something comforting. "I know you don't think so, but you'll get over him. After all, you've only known him two weeks."

Two weeks! The realization shocked Vella. But then it wasn't quite true. She had known him for years. He had been her dream, her vision. She had touched him in the flesh, held him to her, loved him. And now she was expected to forget him.

"Sure, Deb," she said in a thick voice. "Thanks for the use of the cabin. I'll take care of it."

"I know that, Vella. Try to relax."

"Bye, Deb."

"Good-bye, Vella. Be careful."

Vella smiled at the caution. It was too late for her to be careful. She had already been hurt beyond repair. When she had tossed some clothes in a suitcase, she gathered up her painting supplies, her stool, and her newest work and stashed them in her car. After she had retrieved Sneaky, she set out for the isolated mountain cabin.

187

When Matt couldn't locate Vella by the next afternoon, he called Debby.

"Oh, Matt," she said, surprised to hear from him. "How are you?"

"I've been a lot better," he said bluntly. "I can't find Vella. If you know where she is, tell me."

"Gee, Matt—"

"Please, Debby," he said impatiently. "I love her. You've got our future in your hands. I suspect she's confided in you, and you must know how much we love each other."

"But, Matt, I did promise Vella."

"Fine," he said agreeably. "Don't tell me where she went. Just list the possibilities, with the most likely place first. I'll find her."

Sitting in the A-frame cabin in the midst of pine trees, Vella fought to make herself work on the Indian maiden who was the focus of her lilies of the valley card. But every time she looked at the delicate outline of the woman, she saw her own face reflected there, her features soft with the glow of love.

Suddenly she knocked the painting from the easel and buried her face in her hands. How was she going to forget Matt when he was in her mind and heart? When she was reminded of him everywhere she looked?

Drawing her hands from her face, she hugged her arms to her body and began to rock back and forth on the tall stool, trying to find some relief in the physical movement. Her gaze strayed blindly to the view out the window, and she could hardly believe her eyes.

Matt was parking in the driveway! A rush of fury

spiraled up inside her. Damn Debby! She had promised! Vella looked down at the painting that now lay askew on the floor, mocking her. She quickly set it back on the easel and straightened her clothes. There was no point in pretending that she wasn't here. Matt knew better, and, anyway—God help her—her heart danced at the sight of him.

She sucked in her breath when he suddenly burst into the room, not even bothering to knock. "You're a fool, Vella," he declared, striding across the floor to grip her shoulders. "What do you think you're doing? You can't run away from me."

"Oh, Matt," she said weakly, "why don't you just let us get on with our lives?"

"I have every intention of doing that," he insisted. "You're going to marry me."

Shaking her head, Vella moved away. "Why won't you understand that this just won't work?" she cried.

"Why? Because you're a psychic? Because you think it will ruin my chances to be the new California senator? I'm beyond that now, Vella. I know just what to do. I'm going to run for office, no matter what anyone says. If my backers don't like it, I'll go on alone."

He bent his head to touch her lips lightly with his own. "You're my ace in the hole, lady. I'll take you everywhere with me. If my opposition thinks you'll ruin me, wait until they see what really happens when a politician falls in love with a beautiful psychic. The American public will love you. Once they meet you, they'll embrace you as no other politician's wife before you."

Vella felt a foolish spark of hope at his words, but she wasn't naive enough to believe them. "Oh,

Matt, it just won't work. You must realize that."
She turned away from him. "Don't ask me to ruin
you, because that's exactly what will happen if you
want me to go public."

Matt spun her back around. "Trust me. I know
the public will love you. The newspapers want to
give us publicity. Good, we'll let them."

"Matt, you don't know how they can be. For
everyone you try to convince, two will scoff.
Calan—"

"What about Calan?" he demanded, his fingers
biting into her shoulders.

Vella drew in a steadying breath. "Calan
thought he could explain my 'talents' away, too,
but his fellow politicians laughed at him." She
looked away, unable to go on.

"And?" he prompted, not willing to let her stop
now.

Her shimmering gray eyes met his. "He and a
group of politicians were scheduled to fly in a
small plane to Northern California. I had a vision
—" Her words faltered, but she continued: "I had
a vision in which the plane was lost. I tried to tell
Calan, but he was so paranoid about my psychic
abilities by then that he just hung up on me."

Matt stared at her in disbelief for a moment,
thinking how it must have devastated her. "Vella,
Vella, how awful for you," he said, drawing her
close to him. He held her tightly, her head resting
on his shoulder. "Is that the reason for your bitterness toward politics?" he asked. "Calan was too
weak to believe in you because his cronies laughed
at him, and so you blame all politicians for his
loss?"

She drew back from him in mild surprise. He
was right, she realized. That was the reason, yet all

this time she had twisted the facts around in her mind until she believed Calan had been too good, too pure to be involved in politics. But he had been weak. He had refused to see the truth.

"And that's also your fear of being known as a psychic?" Matt asked.

Vella looked into his blue eyes. "Yes. I feel responsible for Calan's death. If he hadn't been involved with me, if he hadn't been ashamed of me being psychic, maybe he would still be alive today."

Matt's voice was very calm and steady. "If he *had* listened to you, *then* he would be alive today, Vella. Not the other way around."

He reached out to stroke her face. "Now you listen to me. I'm not Calan, and I'm not afraid of my backers, or the public, or your psychic talents. I don't want you to change for me. I realize now that your uniqueness is part of what I love about you. I'm going to marry you, and I'm going to continue to run for office."

He smiled at her. "I believe in the people of California. I'll leave it to them to decide if I will be the Republican senator from California. If they don't want me, then I'll do something else—I'll involve myself in some other cause. The love I share with you is the most important thing in my life, and that will see us through."

Vella gazed into his eyes, and she knew that he was telling the truth. No matter what happened, the love they shared, the love that had been born between them long before they met and touched, the love that she knew was to be hers for many years, would live on, rich and secure, beyond the reaches of a curious and sometimes hostile public.

Suddenly Matt's gaze was drawn to the painting

191

of the Indian maiden. There was a peculiar expression on his face, and Vella was concerned.

"What's wrong?" she asked.

He shook his head and blinked his eyes, as if trying to escape from something he couldn't quite believe. "The strangest thing just happened," he said, his dark brow furrowed. "When I looked at that painting, I thought I saw your face among those flowers."

He looked at the painting again and laughed nervously. "Funny, now I only see the face of an Indian girl. You really have driven me mad. *I'm* having visions, but that's all right, as long as you're what I see."

He drew her into his arms and hugged her to him. Vella glanced back at the painting and smiled secretly to herself. Then she lifted her face for Matt's kiss, secure in the knowledge that he was indeed her destiny.